CAPTIVE

CAPTIVE

CLAUDINE DUMONT

Translated by David Scott Hamilton

ARACHNIDE

First published in French under the title *Anabiose* in 2013 by Les Éditions XYZ
First published in English in 2015 by House of Anansi Press Inc.

House of Anansi Press
110 Spadina Avenue, Suite 801
Toronto, ON, M5V 2K4
Tel. 416-363-4343
Fax 416-363-1017
www.houseofanansi.com

House of Anansi Press is committed to protecting our natural environment. As part of our
efforts, the interior of this book is printed on paper that contains 100% post-consumer
recycled fibres, is acid-free, and is processed chlorine-free.

19 18 17 16 15   1 2 3 4 5

Library and Archives Canada Cataloguing in Publication

Dumont, Claudine, 1973–
[Anabiose. English]
Captive / Claudine Dumont ; David Scott Hamilton, translator.

Translation of: Anabiose.
ISBN 978-1-4870-0051-6 (pbk.).—ISBN 978-1-4870-0052-3 (html)

I. Hamilton, David Scott, 1957–, translator II. Title.
III. Title: Anabiose. English.

PS8607.U4445A5213 2015   C843'.6   C2015-902073-5
                                         C2015-902074-3

Book design: Alysia Shewchuk

We acknowledge for their financial support of our publishing program
the Canada Council for the Arts, the Ontario Arts Council, and the Government of Canada
through the Canada Book Fund. We acknowledge the financial support of the Government
of Canada, through the National Translation Program for Book Publishing, an initiative
of the Roadmap for Canada's Official Languages 2013–2018: Education, Immigration,
Communities, for our translation activities.

Printed and bound in Canada

CAPTIVE

I'm looking at the screen, but with the sound off. It's for the light. The illusion of movement around me. I'm afraid of the dark. That's what happens when I drink too much. And I drink too much. Often. And for some time now, even on weeknights. I can't get to sleep without it. I can't forget the empty box of my life without it. The little box. Empty. I don't dare put anything in it anymore. It's not strong enough. The cardboard is brittle. It falls to bits as soon as anyone starts moving it around too much. That's just how it is. I'm not strong enough for life. For my life. A china doll. I'm brittle. No one knows. They mustn't. Fragility is too dangerous. It doesn't take much before others start testing their talent for causing pain. Others. People. Those I know and those I don't. Avoiding them means avoiding pain. It's also a way of avoiding life.

I fell asleep. I dreamt. A dream that comes back often. Always. This dream. I'm in an elevator. There are more than one hundred floors on the control panel. Little black numbers in little illuminated circles. I want to get off. I don't like elevators. In my dreams, they never go where I have to go. They never stop at the floor that I asked for. When I press the button for the lobby, the mechanism fails. The elevator starts falling. The mechanism fails and the elevator falls. I'm inside. Stuck. I'm falling. I know that I'm going to crash. I wake up just before I crash. A dream that I dream often. When I opened my eyes, I was in my bed and darkness was only a few feet away. Ready to crush what was left of me. What encloses me. Sometimes. When I'm not looking. It's just a feeling. I realize that. I'm not one to lose my mind. I can recognize the effects of alcohol. But the feeling is so convincing that I begin to wonder if it's not reality and that the reality that tries to pass itself off as my life, the one that lacks any realism, is a fraud.

The TV is at the foot of my bed. It's a big bed. With lots of pillows. To put one over on the emptiness. But I won't be able to sleep. Another night in my alcoholic fog.

I slept for two hours. That's not bad. I don't work tomorrow. I don't want to think about tomorrow. There's too much space to fill up when I don't work. Too much time to fill in. I need a drink. To increase the fog. To dumb down my thoughts. To stop thinking. My bottle is empty. It's better that way. No, it's not better. There's nothing that's better. Not in my life. Not for a very long time. Nothing better. Just some kind of continuity.

There's a noise in the hallway. I close my eyes for a moment. I can feel the alcohol disturbing my inner balance. I feel sick. I open my eyes. There are two figures in the half-light of my room. One on each side of my bed. Against the light of the television. Dressed in black. In black masks. Am I dreaming? The man to my right. He's speaking into his wrist. Like in the movies. Am I in a movie? He signals to the second man. The man on my left leans towards me. I must have fallen asleep. He grabs my arm. He's hurting me. He pulls me to my feet. In a single movement. I think he says something. I'm not listening. I never really listen. I'm standing. Too quickly. The world is swaying. The man grips my wrists and holds them behind my back. It's uncomfortable. I try to free myself. Without much conviction. I'm dreaming. It won't end. Then it's too much. It's in the excess that everything becomes real. The pain. I never dream of physical pain. I make do with mental torture. That's enough. But now the pain crackles in my wrists. It shoots up my arms. It shatters the fog in my head. Into pieces. A fog of fragments of ice soaked in alcohol. I'm not dreaming. There are two men in my room. Dressed in black. Wearing masks. Armed. The one behind me is still holding my wrists. I can't feel my arms. I can't feel my legs. The walls are going to crash in on me. I can feel the bitter liquid in my stomach rising. I swallow. Hard. Retch. A scream is forming in my stomach. It can't find the exit. The man has just stuck a rag in my mouth. I can't scream. I can't breathe. A chemical smell. I try to move. My legs are made of concrete. I can't move. I try to breathe. I can't breathe. I can't feel my body anymore. My heart. It's beating too fast, too hard. The world fades to black. Then, nothing.

The noise of a motor. No. It's not a motor. A vibration. I try to open my eyes. I can't. I try to move, I can't do that either. I'm tied up. I hear something else. Breathing. No. Whistling. No. Someone is moaning. Is it me? No. It's coming from far away. I don't know anymore. I'm having difficulty concentrating. My head hurts. I can't move. My arms. My legs. Immobilized. There's something cold climbing upwards, encasing my thighs, my stomach, rising, rising, it reaches my neck, it reaches my nose, it's in my head. The cold, the darkness, and then, nothing.

A white light explodes. In my head. Pain. I jump to my feet, shouting. I open my eyes. Unsteady. I'm in an empty room. There are no windows. I'm thirsty. At my feet, there's a mattress. On the bare floor. Grey. Clean. Nothing else. My head is spinning. I fall back onto the mattress. I have no idea where I am. I don't remember how I got here. There's an alarm scream-ing in my head, as violent as the pain. Something's not right. I try to remember. I notice a door at the end of the room. Get out. I get up cautiously. The floor is cold. And clean. My head is spinning. My stomach wants to reject its contents, but I hold back. I swallow. It burns my throat. I want water. I walk towards the door. One foot, the other foot. I realize that my feet are bare. I'm wearing the long-sleeved T-shirt and khaki skirt I threw on for work yester-day. Yesterday. Was it yesterday? Did I sleep for one night? Sleep? No. Not exactly. I try to concentrate, but my thoughts refuse to slip into the machinery of my brain. Everything in there is scattered. I fell asleep. Last night. Well, yesterday. After the tequila. Like always. A lot. To forget. Like always. Why am I here? Another step. One foot, the other foot. I'm thirsty. The wall. The door. Before opening it, I press my forehead against the cold metal. A steel door. I wait. For my heart to calm down. For the alarm in my head to stop screaming. But nothing stops. There is a vague smell of soap. Detergent. No. It smells like a hospital. Disinfectant. Shit. I place my hand gently on the door handle, very gently, as if it were about to explode. I don't know why. Maybe it's the racket from hell that the alarm is making in some dusty recess of my survival instinct, but I turn the handle very carefully. It doesn't budge. At all. Locked. No surprise. I knew it. I was expecting that. The alarm signal screaming in my head isn't in my head. I've been screaming since I got up from that damn mattress. I can't stop screaming and I can't catch my breath. I can't breathe. Now I know. I remember. The men. In my room. My throat has tightened so much that my cries get stuck in it. Silence. Sudden. Finally. My body responds by loosening up. A little. Just enough to let the air escape from my knotted throat. I press my ear against the door. I don't hear anything. The absence of any noise is so enveloping that I feel it against my eardrums. They will come. Motionless, I can hear the beating of my own heart. Too fast. Too hard. They are going to come and kill me. I'm going to die. My heart is racing. I don't want to die. Panic. The more I concentrate on my heartbeat, the more it speeds up. There's nothing else for me to concentrate on. I can't concentrate. Faster, harder. There's pins and needles in my fingertips now. My arms become heavy. My legs are giving way. I fall to my knees. I'm going to pass out. Blackness rises. NO! My stomach clenches. I'm going to pass out. I'm going to vomit. Not in that order. I'm not going to pass out. I. My stomach heaves violently. I vomit. From my mouth, through my nostrils. It burns. The effort keeps the darkness at bay. A second wave of nausea. I feel like I'm vomiting acid. Again. When I vomit, I make an inhuman noise. Sweat coats my body. It smells of something other than my sweat. It's acrid, caustic, almost chemical. It smells of fear. The fear of death. I vomit. Again. It's ripping my stomach apart. Again. The pain. Again. There's nothing left to vomit, but I vomit again. I'm surrounded by a pool of greenish bile. The odour is so strong it stings my eyes. Turns my stomach. Another effort. Another raucous cry. I hurt. I'm scared. Tears of sweat sting my cheeks. Another effort. My stomach is going to burst. I'm going to vomit blood. Another effort, another scream. The pain. I am empty. Blackness.

I open my eyes. I'm on the mattress. Someone has carried me here. I get up slowly. My stomach hurts. My throat hurts. My nose hurts. It hurts to breathe. My head is vibrating. A pain that reverberates incessantly. I am alive. Pain is always a sign of life. There's nothing on the floor. Someone has cleaned it up. The smell of disinfectant. My hair is damp. My clothes are clean. Someone has washed me. I smell of disinfectant, too. I'm thirsty. I need to think. Concentrate. It's difficult above the pain. Above the fear. They came. They haven't killed me yet. I breathe deeply. My ribs hurt, tortured by such effort. I ache. Everywhere. It's the pain that hits the day after. I must have slept. A long time. It's not sleeping. But more like not being here. And they came. And left. Without finishing me off. THEY. I'm thirsty. Incredibly thirsty. It feels like I have sand in my throat. I look around. A huge room. Empty. Nothing but concrete and cement. And the globe of the ceiling light. And the locked door. I get up and lift up the mattress. Cement. Grey.

Everywhere. I walk to the door. I bang on it three times.

"Is anybody there?"

My voice is broken. Rasping.

"Please, I need water."

It's a murmur. That's all I can do. I wait. That's all I can do, too. No sign of movement. I return to the mattress. I sit down. I don't get it. Why me? I'm not important. I don't do anything important. I'm not different enough to make a difference. I'm nothing. Why me? I'm thirsty. I feel like crying. The last time I cried I was six years old. I did something stupid. I can't even remember what it was. My father gave me a spanking. For the first and last time. He bent me over his knee and spanked me six times. Through my pants. It didn't hurt. It humiliated me. I cried in rage. My tears tasted like lead. I never cried again. I'm not going to cry today. Even if I want to. I'm thirsty. I need water. I get up. I walk towards the wall. Concrete. Grey. There aren't even any bumps. Just a flat grey surface. Smooth and even. I walk alongside the walls around the entire room. Nothing. I want to scream, but I don't scream. My throat couldn't handle it. I walk to the centre of the room. Right beneath the globe, there is a drain. I bend down to see if I can lift the grate. The holes are too small for my fingers. I can't do it. I go back to the mattress. I don't know what to do. I'm thirsty. I'm exhausted. I'm too scared to think. It's more than my conscious mind can process. I know that I'm thirsty. Thirsty for water. For tequila, to help me forget. I lie down and close my eyes. My hands are shaking.

I open my eyes. I dreamt that I was drinking water, coffee, juice, milk, tea. I drank tequila, scotch, beer. I drank. Gallons. It wasn't enough. It's never enough. But there is no water. There is no tequila. Nothing. Just grey concrete. And the white globe in the ceiling. My lips are cracked. My tongue is swollen. I'm still thirsty. I still have a headache. My fear is everywhere. Beneath. Hidden. I'm not trying to find it. I don't want to. I'm thirsty. Thirst fills my entire body, my whole head. I feel like a discarded leaf at the end of autumn. Dried out, brittle. Fragile. Dead. They haven't come back. I'm still alive. In one piece. Why? So I can die of thirst?

"Why?"

My voice isn't audible. It doesn't make it across the thickness of the silence. My stomach is swollen. Strained. I need to pee. One thought in this desert. That's what woke me up. How do I do it? If I piss next to the door, will they come and clean it up? Like they did with the vomit? And I can ask them for water.

WATER. Even just a tiny bit. A sip. A drop. But if they don't come back? And if they *do* come back? I'm scared. Too scared. Shhh. My gaze drifts for a moment. I see the drain.

I walk towards it. I'm still aching. I'm having trouble keeping my balance. I can piss down the drain. Seems reasonable. As if there were room for reasonable. Here. Now. I stare at the little holes. My stomach hurts. The urgency makes me almost forget my thirst. Forget my discomfort. Piss in a hole. Forget. I pull off my panties. My skirt. I squat down. I try to urinate on the little perforated grate. I'm alone. I'm still embarrassed. It's stupid. I manage not to splash myself. When I'm done, I'm not sure what to do. I have nothing to wipe myself with. I wait. This is stupid. I wait. I get up and pull my panties back on. I put the skirt back on as well. There's play at my waist. My skirt. There's room between the belt and my stomach. I've lost weight. I think it's more likely the water in my body that I've lost. I want to go back to the mattress. Two steps. I feel dizzy. I sit down on the cool cement. I lie down. I press my cheek against the floor. I'm so thirsty. I have no idea how long I've been locked up in here. More than a day. Perhaps two. Maybe three. If I think too much about it, I can feel my heart racing. I can feel my fear materializing. I don't have the wherewithal to confront it. The fear. I try to think of other things. I know that the body can hold on for three days without water. But I vomited. Three days without water. Three days. I have to concentrate. Three days. Three days. Those two words are taking up all the room in my head. Three days. Three days. THREE DAYS. If I fall asleep, will I wake up? And if they come back when I'm sleeping, will I wake up? I want to live. Do I want to live? I want to live.

I can't sleep. I'm not awake. I wake up, but I haven't slept. I'm thirsty. I'm scared. I'm thirsty. It's no longer thirst. It's gone beyond thirst. It's a state. It's everything I am. Dehydrated. I hear a noise. In the total silence. In the desert. I hear a noise. I want to turn my head, but I can't.

A thought. I manage to concentrate. To wake up. To emerge from the fog. To cross the intangible. Climb back to the surface. Towards reality. Towards fear. I don't want to. Thirst. There was something. I was supposed to do something. A noise. Get up. Turn your head. Open your eyes. Open your eyes. I open my eyes. I'm dreaming. No. Reality. In front of me there is a glass of water. Right there. In front of me. On the cement floor. Water. A glass. A mirage? I have to wake up. No. I have to concentrate. Lift my arm. See if the glass of water is there. In front of me. My fingers make contact with the glass. Cold. Wet. I place my fingers around the glass. It doesn't disappear. I bring the glass closer. Gently. I drag it to me. Gently. I raise my head a little. I don't lift the glass. Afraid to drop it. To knock it over. I place my lips on the rim. I suck the water up. Gently. A tiny sip. On my lips. In my mouth. I swallow. It hurts. It feels like the water is evaporating before it reaches my throat. Is it water? I suck up some more. I swallow. And I swallow water. Real water. The best water I have ever drunk. I suck up some more. Cold. It doesn't taste of anything. Nothing. No metal. No lead. No chlorine. Water. Cold water. Which tastes of nothing. Which tastes of everything. Life. I rest my head for a moment. Just a tiny moment.

I raise myself up and take a real sip. A little one. I'm afraid of choking. I'm afraid it will disappear. I can feel the water descending to my stomach. Moistening everything in its path. It's an extraordinary sensation. I drink another sip. Water. A treasure. I close my eyes. Two seconds. Three seconds. I want more. I open my eyes. Another sip. I close my eyes. For an instant, I forget where I am. I forget that I exist. I feel only immense satisfaction. Complete satisfaction. Water. I open my eyes. The glass is almost empty. And what if I have to wait as long for the next glass of water? And what if there is no next time? I get up on my knees. My head is spinning. I sit back on my haunches. Breathe. There's a slight fog around me, but the room remains stable. Grey, concrete, mattress, ceiling globe. Nothing is moving. I look at the glass of water. The desire to drink the last two sips overwhelms everything. My logic. My thoughts. My body. My heart. I have never heard my heart before. It never beat loud enough. It's the silence. It finds its place in silence. I can hear it. Not just beating, but pounding out the rhythm of this howling desire: two sips of water. I want to drink. I'm paralyzed. By the memory of what happened eight minutes ago. By my reality eight minutes ago. The reality in which there was no water. The reality in which there will be no more water. I stay where I am. I watch. I don't move. The silence in my head. Forget the fear. The silence. And water.

I'm trying to understand. I'm killing myself trying to understand. My headache's gone. I held out for the two sips. I spent a whole day watching the glass without moving. I think it was a day. It probably wasn't a whole day. When I began to feel sleepy, I drank the two sips and I lay down. On the mattress. When I woke up, there was a pitcher of water. I was careful, but I drank it all before feeling sleepy again. When I opened my eyes, there was a new pitcher. With the old one. One with water, the other with a mixture that tasted of lemon and salt. I drank it all. Today, if it's actually daytime, I have no idea, the two pitchers are there, full once again. I'm feeling better. But it's not better. The silence. The absence of time. The fear. Always. Constant. Exhausting. Questions without answers. The silence. The four concrete walls, the mattress, the silence. And nothing else.

I walk along the walls. I lie down on the mattress. I go to the drain. And I wait. I wait, but I don't know what I'm waiting for. All I can do is the very thing I don't want to do. Look back. Think. Speculate. Why are they keeping me alive? Theft, rape, kidnapping, nothing makes sense. And I have nothing. And my parents have nothing. Well, at least nothing that's worth my abduction. The only thing I have is myself. My body. Yesterday, if it was yesterday, I thought about organ trafficking. That didn't make any sense either. I examined myself. Nothing. No stitches. Nothing. I told myself that they were holding me until some rich guy needed me. Emergency organs for the failing bodies of the rich. Organ carrier. It's such an abominable scenario that I can't bring myself to believe it. Not exactly. And then there's the other scenario. The white slave trade. I'm white. I'm twenty-six years old. I'm too old. At least I think I am. I don't know. Probably not. The white slave trade. Words that sum up the inhuman in the human. But why the wait? And why am I here? Why don't I see anyone else? Why am I locked up? Why am I not somewhere else? Why?

I want a bottle of tequila. But there's nothing here. I want to know. I want to forget. I'm scared. I'm trying not to be afraid. It paralyzes me. I'm scared I'll go crazy. I play hide-and-seek in my own brain. I hide the fear as far away as possible. I don't go looking for it. But it's there. Everywhere. Fear. Horror. Terror. Anguish. Panic. In every recess. Like starving wild animals ready to pounce. Ready to dine on what's left of my logic. I must not think about it. I mustn't look. But the whys keep coming back. Why here, why me? Why, why, WHY! There's no answer. Only concrete. Grey.

Another day. I think. How long before someone notices my absence? I see my parents twice a year. And I saw them last month. They'll start worrying in six months. No one will notice anything at work. A missing customer service representative isn't exactly noticeable when the company employs more than four thousand. And people don't stay long. Except for me. In the five years that I've worked there, the cubicle to my right has seen roughly thirty employees come and go. The one to my left, twice that number. It's a job that eventually softens your brain. No one bothers to give two weeks' notice. They just stop coming. That's all. And Human Resources replaces them. There's undoubtedly someone already doing my job, taking calls from unsatisfied customers. And there's no end to that dissatisfaction. I have some friends I rarely see that I haven't seen at all for some time. Ex-boyfriends I no longer talk to. There's not even a putrefying cat in my apartment to alert the neighbours. I'm the girl who can disappear without a ripple. As if I didn't really belong to society. A nonparticipating member of humanity. Insignificant, whether present or absent. Not exactly a revelation.

I'm banging on the door. With my fist. For how long? My fist hurts. I start banging again. I don't think I even inhabit this body that's banging a fist against a steel door. Stubborn. This is stupid. They don't answer.

I open my eyes. I have no idea how I even manage to sleep. I'm not tired. I don't do anything. I try not to think about what's going to happen next. That's all I do. Relentlessly. Try not to think that nothing will ever happen. That everything will stay the same. An unending string of empty moments. An eternity. I drink, I piss, I walk around in circles, I don't think, I sleep. There's no reason for me to wake up. There's no reason for me to sleep. I'm not sure if I've gotten used to fear, or if fear is no longer necessary, but I'm less afraid. I open my eyes, grey concrete. Always grey concrete. I'm not afraid of grey concrete. And the pitchers of water are always full. There has to be something in the lemon-scented pitcher, because I'm not hungry at all. I dream about eating. About putting something solid in my mouth. Chewing. Tasting. Smelling. Cinnamon buns. Some bread and cheese. French fries with way too much salt. A greasy hamburger. Anything. When I think about it, my mouth fills with saliva. I salivate like a dog. I miss eating.

But I'm not starving. I feel like drinking alcohol, but not really. There's nothing here to avoid. I don't need to fog up my mind. It's more like desire out of habit. Comfort. But not really.

I don't get up anymore. I lie on the mattress. I open my eyes. I close my eyes. I don't dream anymore. I'm not sure if I sleep. I drift. Conscious, unconscious. But it's always grey. And time doesn't pass. Nothing changes. A hell in which nothing happens and nothing moves. As if I were already dead. Something has to change. I need something to mark the passage of time. So I don't go crazy. I close my eyes. I have a dream. I dream that I can see myself sleeping on the mattress. The grey mattress. On the grey cement. And my body turns grey. The floor, the mattress, me: a mass of grey. Motionless. Petrified. I wake up. I don't want to disappear. I don't want to die. I can move. I must move. I will move. Do some exercise. Like those guys in prison who bulk up because they have nothing else to do. Am I in prison? I'm going to exercise. I have nothing to lift, but I still have my body. My body is all I have. I get up. I take a drink. I take off my skirt and start stretching. Then some sit-ups. Not too many. I'm quickly exhausted. I do some squats. My thighs are burning. I keep going. I try some push-ups. I do two. I can't do more. Then I start running. In a circle. Barefoot. Like a rat in a cage. I'm not in prison. I'm in a cage. I run. I stop to have a drink. I feel a little better. I'm hot, there's sweat on my face, the underarms of my shirt are soaking wet. I can smell sweat. Just sweat. Not death. A reassuring smell. It smells like life.

I open my eyes. I have something to do. I get up. I drink some water. I ache all over. I didn't know that pain could make me feel good. I drink the lemon-scented water. A different taste. I don't stop. I stretch. I push through the pain. It feels good. I do the same thing I did yesterday. I run in a circle.

It's morning, or perhaps it's not, but it's my morning. My hair is damp. My clothes smell of disinfectant. They're washing my clothes. They wash me. I realize that I haven't passed any stool since I've been here. Enemas? They're cleaning my insides as well? How do they do that without waking me up? The water. They must be putting something in the lemon water. I can feel a kind of rebellion forming inside me. They're cleaning out my insides. They're drugging me. THEY. A knot in my stomach. Then nothing. What can I do? I'm not going to stop drinking. My exercises. My skirt is too big. I don't have to unzip the zipper to take it off. I'm not sure why I continue to wear it. It's not cold in here. It's must be something else. Rats don't wear skirts. But they run when they're cooped up. They run around in circles. I'm not a rat. I place my skirt on the mattress. I run. In circles.

I don't hurt when I get up anymore. No more nausea, no more headache. No more ache in my muscles. No more pain. Not even fear. I can do fifty push-ups. But no more than that. I prefer to run. I can run for what seems like hours. There is something in the lemon water. Which allows me to do all that. Without eating. I'm sure of it. The taste is different. I know when they're going to wash me, too. The taste of the sleeping pill through the lemon has become evident. I can choose not to drink. I don't. I run. While I'm running, I don't think of anything. My thighs have changed. My body has changed. I know it. It marks the passage of time. I know it, but I don't see it. I can't see myself. I haven't seen myself since. Since. I pat myself to ensure I'm still here. But I can't see myself reflected in the grey concrete. The globe on the ceiling is too high to return my reflection. The pitchers are made of plastic. A material that reflects nothing. And there is no one to tell me. No one.

I'm used to the absence of others. I always sought isolation. Before. I built it around me. They weighed too heavily on me. Others. They caused me pain. With their looks, their questions. Their expectations. Their disappointments. I'd had enough. I didn't want to see myself in their eyes anymore. Their image of me. The image of who I no longer was. I couldn't tell them. Too difficult. Too complicated. I lacked the words. And if I found the words, no one wanted to hear them. Not really. They kept clashing with the old version of me. I would say, "I don't want to be here." Someone would say, "Come on, you love this, of course you want to be here." I didn't love it. Not for a very long time. But no one listened. No one listens to change. I couldn't act any other way. And I no longer knew who I was. I no longer knew what to say. I decided not to say anything anymore. I avoided people. No one really noticed. Same thing at work. My job. I wouldn't dare do anything else. Working in an isolated cubicle, with only the voices of the dissatisfied, no one looking at me. Just floating voices that protest, demand, scream. Which don't touch me. I say nothing. I can do that. I do it well. And then I go home, my mind at rest. Home, I miss my home. A home for me. No cat. No one. Just tequila. To forget. And kill time. While I wait. I was waiting for things to change. I think I was. Without doing anything to bring about the change. Things. People. Now, things have changed. There aren't any things. There aren't any people. Nothing to avoid. Just me. And me. With me. And I forget. It's more effective than tequila. I forget who I was. Why I avoided things. I can't remember. A girl. Who drank. Too much. Who worked. Like an automaton. Who lived. Barely. Like an automaton. Who avoided. Who was afraid. That fear was nothing. It was the fear of my own shadow. Brought on by pride. By shame. Humiliation. Failure. It doesn't really exist. It's all in your head. In my head. In the heads of others. Unreal. It doesn't exist anymore. Not here. Here, there's nothing. Do I really exist when there's nothing? I exist. I live. I move. I'm not waiting anymore. There's nothing to wait for. Freed from expectation. Nothingness. The void. But there is still a desire for life. A desire not to die. A desire not to go crazy. To keep control of my mind. Of my thoughts. To want. Is that enough? I am not going to concede.

I open my eyes. There's this thought. Always my first thought. I think about tomorrow, which will be the same. As today. No change. Ever. A stream of unbearable days. Identical. I refuse this thought. I can't think like this. It paralyzes me. I push the thought far back in my mind, behind a grey concrete wall. I get up. I concentrate on the next minute. The next second. I take a drink. I take off my skirt. I pitch it at the mattress. It misses. It hits the wall. I leave it. I run. I'm exhausted. I run all the same. When my lungs start to burn, I stop thinking. I don't stop running. When I can't go any further, I run a little more, and then I stop. A vague feeling of accomplishment. At least it's something. As I bend down to pick up my skirt, I notice a mark on the wall, probably from the metal tab of the zipper. I take the tab between my fingers, the skirt hanging below my hand, and start scratching the wall. The concrete crumbles a little. Not much. But a little. A mark. I can make a mark. I sit down on the mattress. A world of possibilities. A mark. My hands are shaking. I kneel down in front of the wall. I hold the metal tab between my fingers. I make a line. A curve. My heart starts beating faster. I draw another line. It doesn't mean anything, but it's something to do. I start laughing. The sound of my own laughter scares me. I stop.

I'm lying on the mattress. It's night. My night. I'll fall asleep soon. It hits like a wave. Sleep. I look at the wall. It's covered in little roads. They cross each other, branch out, wriggle and squirm. They're magnificent. When I started, I had blisters on my fingers. Calluses now. And then I was afraid the metal tab would break. Wear down. That didn't happen. I look at this drawing, which isn't a drawing. It's magnificent. A work of incredible detail. It took forever. I think it did. Methodical work. Repetitive. Compulsive. It amounts to nothing. It's magnificent. The work of a deranged mind? Shhh. There are still three walls left. And that fills me with an indescribable joy. I close my eyes. I will sleep now. Satisfied. Run and draw. I float between these two states of consciousness. A thought is trying to surface. It escapes me. Like a cloud that forms a shape that I don't have time to recognize before it turns into something else. I let the cloud envelop me. Then I see it. The thought. Which I don't want to see. Or hear. Or understand. I'm happy. Locked up.

Isolated. Cut off from the rest of the world. Locked up. But the wall, the drawing makes me happy. Am I broken in? Have I adapted? Am I tamed? I can feel tears flowing down my cheeks. That's impossible. I must already be sleeping.

I hear a noise. Irregular breathing. It's not me. I open my eyes. I turn my head around. There's another mattress. Someone is sleeping on that mattress. I straighten up. I hold my breath. I don't move. Am I dreaming? Am I hallucinating? I close my eyes. I breathe very lightly. Quietly. I try to calm the beating of my heart. I open my eyes. He's still there. He's breathing. There's a slight whistle to his breathing. A sound. I don't dare move. I watch him sleep. I'm scared. What is he doing here? He's lying on his back. An arm under his head. His other hand rests on his stomach. He's wearing grey jeans. A black T-shirt. His feet are bare. His hair is dark. His beard looks a few days old. He's sleeping. I'm afraid of him. I'm afraid. It's not the same fear I had at the beginning, fear of dying. That was real fear. Maybe this should be, too. He's going to wake up and everything will be different. He's going to see me. He's going to. What is he doing here? Why did they put him in here?

"No."

My voice. A whisper. He stirs. In his sleep. I don't want him here. I want to make him disappear. Before he wakes up. Before it's too late. I want to kill him. Choke him. So he's no longer here. It's simple. An instinctive reaction to a threat. Is this a threat? Can I kill? To stay alive? To survive. This urgency confuses me. It's suffocating me. It's paralyzing me. Hurry. HURRY! But do what? How? I don't have to look around. I know there's nothing here. I take a look anyway. I look. Around me. Something. A weapon. A solution. Something. Maybe on him. A belt? I turn around. He's sitting up. He's watching me. I freeze. Silence.

He looks older awake. There's something world-weary in his eyes. His mouth is hard. His cheeks are hollow. He's clenching his teeth. Hard. His jaw is a rigid square. Tense, nervous. He makes a movement towards me. I back up. Instinct. His eyes widen. With surprise. I think. He opens his mouth to speak. I tell him not to. No. With my head. He stops. He looks around. He takes in the wall. My wall. The one with all the roads, the one with my drawing. And then turns back to me. Something has relaxed. In his face. He's a little less frightening. He takes a deep breath. He opens his mouth. He's going to say something. I don't want him to. I don't know why. I don't want him to.

"Are you okay?"

His voice is deep. Baritone. Cold. A vibration. I don't know what to say.

"I don't know."

A murmur. My vocal cords are rusty, unused. Not his. He tilts his head to the side. The way you look at a child.

"Are you in pain?"

Pain? No. I'm not in pain. Not for a long time. Not physically.

"No."

"Have you been here for a long time?"

Questions. They give me a headache. I don't want questions. I don't want him to be here. I want them to take him back. He's exhausting me.

"I think so."

He exhales. Heavily. He closes his eyes. His forehead is creased. He lifts his hand and runs it up the side of his face. He opens his eyes.

"What's your name?"

I don't answer. I notice the scars on his forearms. Recent wounds, healed. Little mounds of white skin. But wounds. Lots of them. He follows my gaze. Crosses his arms to hide the scars. He doesn't repeat his question. He looks at me. In the eyes. It feels like he's looking past my eyes, into my head. I don't like it. I don't want it. I want to run. I want to draw on the other wall. I want him to leave. To disappear. Here. Now. Immediately. But he's looking at me and doesn't disappear. He runs his hand through his hair. He extends his arms and shows me his scars.

"I tried to escape. Have you tried to escape?"

I start choking. What does that mean? They punished him? He tried to escape and hurt himself? He tried to die? Something in my head wants to give way, wants to abandon the illusion that my thoughts have any coherence, wants to howl. I haven't tried to escape. I didn't even think of it. I didn't even think of it once. It was an impossibility. I didn't think of it. How is it possible that I didn't try, didn't think about it? I'm convinced that it wouldn't have changed anything. But not even a thought? I didn't even think of it. I lower my eyes. I feel like I've made a mistake. Because I didn't even try. A feeling that hasn't shown up to rot inside me for a long time. Incompetence. And for that, I hate him. It rises like a huge wave. A flood. A projection. I want him to disappear.

"No."

My voice is a bite. A bark. He looks at me. He heard. What I didn't say. He hears it. He raises an eyebrow. He grits his teeth. He gets up. He picks up his mattress and places it by the wall. Not the one with the drawings. The other one. The one that faces the door. Then he sits down, his back pressed against the wall. He takes a look around the room, stops at the globe on the ceiling, and then comes back to me. He says nothing. I don't know what to do. I feel like running. I don't dare. I feel like running and then drawing right after. But that's impossible. Because of him.

He doesn't move. He looks at the globe. He looks at me. His head doesn't move. Only his eyes. I don't move. I'm sitting on my mattress. I say nothing. The silence doesn't bother me. He's watching me. His expression is hard. His calm is just a facade. Fragile. The tension in his muscles betrays everything that's going on beneath that false repose. The silence bothers him. I bother him. Anger. I know this reaction. I've seen it many times. I never know what to do with the anger of others. When it's not directed at me, I don't do anything. I wait for it to pass. When it *is* directed at me, I don't do anything. I wait for it to pass. That's not an adequate response. I can't do anything else. I can't confront such intense emotion. It's too difficult. Too detrimental. The potential for emotional injury. Words that outstrip thought. The impossibility of keeping control. I can't respond to that. I close in on myself and wait for it to pass. That's not an adequate response. It's what I do.

The tension doesn't diminish. I can feel it. It's there. Everywhere. It's coming from him. I'm being subjected to his tension. There's no way I can extract myself from it. I don't move. He doesn't move. I wait. I close my eyes. I imagine that I'm running. The motionless muscles of my legs fill up with the sensation of running. I forget the tension. His tension. In my head, I'm running. The weirdest thing is that even in my head, I'm running in the same grey room, round and round in circles.

"It's ridiculous."

His voice makes me jump. I open my eyes. He's standing. Stock-still. His hands in the pockets of his jeans. His feet spread. His toes look like they're planted in the cement. He's looking at me. He doesn't look threatening. His shoulders. His shoulders are relaxed. His chin is raised, proud, but that appears to be habit. He's no longer angry. He's waiting. I want to ignore him. I mutter a response.

"Well, ridicule never killed anybody."

A look of surprise.

"God, why would I kill you?"

I'd do it, if I could, just to get rid of him. I think I would. Maybe. To be free of him. Free? In this concrete cage? Free of him. I realize it's ridiculous. I say nothing. He starts walking. He walks as if nothing could stop him. Nothing. Ever.

"What did you use to do that?"

He points to the drawing on the wall. I show him the metal tab from my skirt. He nods.

"It's very... detailed. Beautiful. Meticulous. Are you going to continue?"

I don't answer right away. I look at him. I'm wondering what has happened in his head to completely change his body language. There are no more non-verbal threats.

"I have to take my skirt off."

To run. To draw. I have to take my skirt off.

"Oh."

He raises an eyebrow. And a corner of his mouth lengthens. Like a tiny smile. But he doesn't say anything else. He sits back down. On his mattress. He rests his arms on his tucked-up knees. His hands hang freely in space. The index finger and thumb of his right hand are rolling an invisible ball.

"I've been looking for something to mark time. I never thought of my jeans."

The half smile on his lips. I don't even remember which muscles to move to make a smile.

"Why are you here?"

My voice is shaky, barely audible, as if it might break. He looks at me. Surprised.

"Do you know why *you're* here?"

There's hope in his voice.

"No. I mean you, why are you here, in my room."

I said MY room. The notion of possession seems absurd. And important.

"A lack of available cages? What do I know..."

He watches me for a moment. He doesn't say anything else. He closes his eyes. I don't dare get up. I stay on my mattress. The idea of an unending chain of nothing, and now with this onlooker weighing over me, is unbearable. I curl up in a ball. I don't close my eyes. I'm not tired and I don't know if I'll be able to sleep with this guy in my room. I hear him get up. I raise my head. I pull back. He walks over to the pitcher of water. He sighs.

"I'm not going to hurt you."

The expression on his face is calm. I believe him.

"Do you want some water?"

I shake my head. He takes a drink.

"Do you mind telling me your name?"

I shake my head.

He sighs again, shrugs, and goes back to his

mattress. I lie back down, but I keep my eyes open. And on him.

I fell asleep. I didn't want to, but I didn't take whatever they put in the water into account. I sit up. He's still sleeping. The whistle in his breathing. I wait. I should try something. While he's sleeping. So they come and get him. I can't find anything, any suitable object. There's nothing I can do. He starts to stir. If I could, I'd knock him out. He is less present when he sleeps. There's not a big difference between sleep and unconsciousness. I've got nothing. I'm not strong enough. He opens his eyes. He sits up.

"Hey!"

I don't respond. He doesn't press me. He gets up, walks over to the pitcher for a drink. I'm not his concern. I keep my eyes on him. He sits down, his back to the wall and looks at the globe. His hair looks damp. They washed him last night. Not me. His week-old beard is gone. They shaved him. I realize that they've been shaving me too. My legs. My armpits. I hadn't noticed. They're tidying me up. Even my nails. Indecent. That's the only word that comes to me. It's indecent. I try to add it all up. Kidnapping. Illegal confinement. Shaving. I can't do anything about it. I feel like I have a bowling ball in my stomach. Me asleep. Them grooming me like a dog. More like a lab rat. I feel sick. Too aware. I don't want it. I don't want this. I can't do anything. Forget. Pretend as if. I breathe in. I breathe out. Our eyes meet.

"How many times have you had your period since you've been here?"

What?

"What?"

"It might give us an idea of how much time has gone by."

Us? There's no *us*. There's him, there's me. I don't want any "us." I don't answer him. I'm confused. I hadn't realized it, but I haven't had one. That's crazy. Have I stopped bleeding?

"Not once."

"Do you think you've been here for less than a month?"

"No. I think I've stopped menstruating."

"Hmm."

He doesn't say anything else. I'm suddenly caught up in all his questions. They keep insisting. Pushing. Rushing. Again. How could I not notice that my period had stopped? What are they doing to me? What are they putting in the water? Is it because I'm not eating? Why? I feel like drinking something. Scotch. Tequila. I feel like. I feel like. I FEEL LIKE. I haven't felt that desire since... since here. I want silence in my head. I push the questions out. I look up at the concrete wall. I pile them all behind it. I want room in my consciousness. I want. He moves. I don't want any more questions. I curl up in a ball and bury my head in my arms. I make him disappear.

He's still here. I try to reason with myself. I try to act as if I were alone. I can't. I can't do it. I feel like running. I don't dare. I feel like drawing. I don't dare. I don't know who he is. Why did they put him in here? With me. I feel like a prisoner in my own prison. It's ridiculous. But that's how it feels. His presence limits my freedom even more than the four grey walls of this room. He wakes up. He sits up. Runs a hand through his hair. He greets me with a nod. I don't respond. He goes to get some water. He takes up too much space. He takes up all the space. I don't know how he does it. It's what he exudes. Impatience. Irritation. Anger. He walks as if each one of his steps were crushing one of *them*. He vibrates. That's it. He vibrates like an overloaded circuit breaker about to trip. He doesn't turn towards me, but begins to speak.

"We have to provoke them."

Provoke. Break the cycle. What would be the point of that? How could I be of any use?

"That would only make things worse."

He turns around. Stares straight into my eyes. The expression on his face is a rebuke. Like a slap. I recoil.

"Worse than being locked up in this holding cell?"

There is so much worse than this. How could he not know that?

"They might stop filling the pitchers."

He stops. He wasn't moving, but he stops. He stops taking up all the space. For a fraction of a second, he is smaller. He studies me. His voice is cautious.

"Have they taken the water away from you before?"

Another expression. Different. I don't answer. I watch him. He waits. He gives me time.

"The first few days, there was nothing."

"What?"

"There was no water."

"For days?"

"Yes."

He closes his eyes. He exhales. I understand that it was different for him. He didn't experience thirst. Why me and not him?

I can feel his anger resurface. Physically, it's visible. The muscles in his jaw have contracted. His back is straight. His fists. The effort to maintain control. The air is charged, heavier. My chest suddenly feels oppressed. Reaction. Break the escalation before there's an explosion. Do something. Say something. Quick.

"First there was just a glass. Then a pitcher. Then the other one."

I can hear everything I don't say in my voice. He can hear it too. He's restless. He begins to expand. As though he were being inflated. He reoccupies all the space. He crushes me. Checkmate.

"And you didn't do anything?"

Do what? He talks like there were other possibilities. I didn't get the impression that I had a choice. I didn't get the impression of choice. At any time.

"I hold on, that's all I can manage."

He looks at me. From the height of his six feet. He seems so tall that it makes me dizzy. He starts walking again. It isn't walking. It's something else. It's more like he's searching for something. Something to bite into.

"Hold on until what?"

He clenches his fists. He goes up to the door. He comes back, towards me. He's not looking at me.

"Do you really think they'll let you go home? If you're a good little girl?"

He's hurting me. My voice is tiny.

"I don't know. I didn't think of it like that."

Not exactly like that, but I realize that yes, in a certain way. Hope.

He's angry. With me. It's visible in his entire body. Why?

"Listen, little girl..."

Little girl? There isn't even ten years between us.

"What's happening here doesn't respect rules. Things aren't going to turn out fine just because you play nice. What do you imagine? Some kind of justice?"

"Stop."

I whisper. I don't feel like listening to what he has to say. I don't want to look behind the concrete wall in my head. I want to hold on. He doesn't hear me. He keeps going.

"We have to do something, it's the only way to get out of here. It's not like anybody is coming to get us."

I don't answer. I can't. I think he's right. I think I'm waiting for justice. That's what I was always taught. At home, at school. If you do the right thing, you'll succeed. If you put in the necessary effort, you'll succeed. There's an intrinsic justice to life. But it's not true. I suddenly let an entire system of thought collapse in my head. That's what I've been pushing back behind the wall of my consciousness since I've been here. He got water. Straight away. Not me. Why?

"I'm not going to wait around for death with my arms crossed. So you can keep holding on if you want to. I..."

I don't say anything. I can't take this anymore. I don't want to hear him anymore. I can't even think of death. I don't want to. I'm trying to hate him. Him. But I can't. Not exactly. I know he's right. At least I've got that. A semblance of reason. He got water. Why? I'm trying to maintain the illusion that things can change by themselves, that my situation can improve. That this madness will end and order will resume its natural course. I'm trying. I can't do it. Because of him. His words. His presence.

"Enough."

A murmur. I don't add anything else. But he hears me. He stops. I need a moment. I can feel tiny drops of sweat on my temples. On my forehead. On the crest of my upper lip. Breathe.

He walks towards my mattress. I can hear him. I don't want to open my eyes. I don't want to lift my head. He touches my shoulder. Just barely. I open my eyes. I raise my head. He's squatting down. So he's the same height as me. His eyes are worried.

"I'm sorry."

I have nothing to say. I can't exactly answer with "That's okay, I'm fine." I close my eyes. Avoidance. I can hear him changing position. He lets the silence float for a moment. Then his voice, controlled, deep, prudent.

"But we still have to do something."

I open my eyes. He's sitting. His long legs stretched out in front of him. He's staring off into space. He's giving me space. I can breathe.

"We have to do something."

He's completely convinced of it.

I don't hear him breathing. I open my eyes. I sit up. He's still there. He's sleeping. But I don't hear him breathing. I walk softly towards him, not making a sound. Maybe he's dead. I lean down very slowly. I don't want him to wake up. I watch him. He's sleeping on his back. He looks younger with his eyes closed. His mouth is half-open. His torso rises. He's breathing. I realize that I'm relieved. I don't want him dead. I'm not sure why. I just want him not to be here. Then he opens his eyes. I back up too suddenly. I lose my balance. His eyes open wide. He's on his feet before I hit the concrete. Without a sound. Silence. There's too much silence. He's speaking to me. I can see that he's yelling. I don't hear anything. He stops. He claps his hands. I don't hear anything. I don't hear anything. I shake my head. He brings his fingers to his ears. He shakes his head. He shows me his ears. He can't hear a thing. I can't hear a thing. I mouth, "No." I scream. I can feel a vibration in my throat, but I can't hear a thing. He's standing. He's looking at me. He doesn't move. He can't move. I can't find the strength to get up. A thousand thoughts rush through my head at an impossible speed. I feel like I'm going to implode. My fingers begin to go numb. I recognize panic. The tightening in my throat, my stomach contracting. The cold in my fingers and toes. No. I don't want to lose consciousness. Not now. There must be something in my eyes, on my face, because I can see something in his. He leans down, takes hold of my shoulders, and pulls me to my feet. Brutally. I feel weak, I grab onto his forearms. I stay standing. He holds my shoulders. I hold his arms. His nose is only a few centimeters away from mine. On his lips I read: *breathe*. He breaks down the sounds. *Br...ee...the*. I take in a huge breath. He exhales with me. His breath is hot on my face. It smells slightly of lemon. He looks around. He's still holding me. I concentrate. Breathe. I can't hear my heartbeat slowing down. But I can feel it. I close my eyes. He shakes me. I open my eyes. He's looking at me. Worry in his eyes. I nod my head. I'm here. I'll make it.

He lets go of me, leaves his hands close to my shoulders, ready to catch me if I fall. I let go of him. I breathe. He takes a step backwards. He catches my attention, points the index and middle fingers of his right hand at his eyes, then at my ear. He wants to look in my ears. I push my hair back behind my ear and lean my head forward. He's taller than me. He has to bend down. He gives me a sign to show him the other ear. I obey. He turns me a little towards the light. Pulls on my earlobe. Then lets me go. He shakes his head. Nothing. No operation to remove our hearing. Then he points his finger at the globe on the ceiling and mimes an injection. An injection? The globe? Them? He starts looking at his arms. He pulls off his T-shirt and scrutinizes his torso. He looks for a mark, a trace of an injection. He turns around and points to his back. I move closer and look at every square inch of his back. I lift his hair to examine his neck. A shiver crosses his skin when I touch him. I step back, but I don't withdraw my hand. I check behind his ears, I find nothing. He turns back around. I shake my head. He starts to undo his pants. I feel ridiculous, but I turn my head. I mask my embarrassment by studying my arms, my hands, my fingers. I don't see anything. I scrutinize my thighs, my legs, my feet, my toes. Nothing. I try to ignore the absence of any sound when I move. I raise my eyes. He's looking at me. The question is in his eyes. I shrug my shoulders. He runs a hand up the side of his face, and then puts his pants back on. He goes back and sits on his mattress. He looks at the globe. There is so much hatred in his face. No word can capture that expression. When something happens, I get scared. And then I panic.

And then I get used to it. But he gets furious. He hates. Ferociously. The hatred of an animal. I don't think he'll adapt. I don't think he'll get used to this. I look at the white lines on his arms. Never.

I open my eyes. I can't hear anything. He's sleeping. I can't hear his breathing. I'm still deaf. Forever? I don't think about it. I avoid the thought. I don't get up. I don't know what to do. I watch him. He wakes up. He sits up. He looks at me. He points to his ears. I shake my head. No sound. He gets up to drink some water. He returns to his mattress. Back against the wall. Eyes on the globe. I look up at the globe. Then I get it. How they know. The globe. I hadn't thought of that. I didn't even ask myself the question. They're watching us. Obviously. The globe is the only place to hide something. There's nowhere else. He knew it. He thought of it. Him. His habit of staring at the light without blinking his eyes. He's known for a long time. I move closer and sit down beside him. On his mattress. I look at the light. I don't see anything. Just white. Too much white. But I sit there, my eyes riveted to the light. Even if it hurts. Just for not having thought of it before. Then I see it. Sections of white that are less than white. Grey. A shadow moving inside. At the globe's centre. I turn to him. I can't see him. I see a huge patch of light. I close my eyes. The white ball remains imprinted on my retinas. I wait for it to disappear. I open my eyes. He's looking at me. I take his arm and turn the inside of his forearm upwards. I write an *E*. I form the sound with my lips. *E*. Then I do the same thing for each letter in my name. I pronounce the name in separate syllables. Em-ma. Emma. He smiles at me. It seems easy for him. To smile. He takes my arm and writes *Julian*. I mouth, "Julian." He raises a thumb. Understood.

I get up. I need water. I head towards the pitchers. Just water. Not the one with the protein supplement. When I lift the pitcher to my lips, Julian appears and holds my arm back. I jump. I set it back down. He points a finger at the water and plugs his ears. Something in the water? I don't think so. It doesn't taste like anything. I make him understand this. I touch my tongue. I shake my head. I point to the protein water. I shrug my shoulders. Maybe. I take a sip anyway. I sit back down. I can't stay stationary. It's worse. The silence on top of the lack of movement. I start walking. In circles. Like when I run. I walk. I don't look at Julian. I look at my feet. I try to forget the silence. I walk faster and faster. I forget Julian. His presence. His anger. I start running. I can't hear my breathing accelerate. I try not to think about it. My skirt is bothering me. I stop. I take it off. I toss it on my mattress. I go back to running. I run faster. I concentrate on the air entering my lungs, leaving my mouth. Without a sound. I concentrate on my feet, which don't make any noise when they hit the cement. I feel each blow. Each step reverberates in my knees, in my spine. In my skull. I think of a song. To keep my thoughts occupied. To fill the silence. "Run Like Hell" by Pink Floyd. First the music, then the words. *You'd better run.* My brain *can* be logical. I run with my eyes closed. I know my route by heart. I run right up to the point where my feet beg me to stop. First I slow down, then I walk and I stop. I come back. To the silence. I look up. Julian is watching me. I should be embarrassed. I'm not. There's no judgement. On his lips, I read the question, "Does it help?" I mouth a yes. He gives me a thumbs-up. He gets up. He takes a deep breath. He starts running.

He takes my route. I go back to my mattress. I pull my skirt on. I sit down and I watch him run. I count. At the beginning, when I started running, I counted all the time. It helped me think of nothing. I know how many seconds it takes me to do a lap around the room. It takes him a little less. His legs are long. His strides are stubborn. There's nothing uncertain about him. Watching him run is almost as liberating as running myself. Hypnotizing. Truly something to see. Something to keep my brain busy. Even without a soundtrack, it's a distraction. An effortless absence of thought. Entertainment.

A shower. Hot. The sensation of water. The smell of soap. A tiny detail from daily life. I wake up with this need on my skin. There is no shower. There is no hot water. There's silence. And the Other. I watch him sleeping. He's peaceful. When his eyes open, it's a different story.

I haven't opened my eyes yet. My consciousness registers silence. Another night. Nothing has changed. I open my eyes. I turn my head towards Julian. He's sleeping. On his back. An arm under his head. He goes to sleep like that. He wakes up in the same position. He sleeps without moving. I ask him, "Do you hear me?" He doesn't wake up. I can't hear myself. Nothing has changed. We tried not to drink anything yesterday. Not the water or the protein drink. I am parched, and I can't hear anything. I get up and I have a drink. I take advantage of the fact that he's sleeping to urinate. I have no idea why, but I always wake up before him. Maybe he falls asleep after me. I sit up on my mattress and wait for him to wake up. The rhythm of his breathing changes when he starts waking up. I can see the rise and fall of his rib cage quicken. He opens his eyes. I can see his lips moving. He does the same thing as me. Maybe he doesn't say the same thing, but it's still the same. He sits up and gives me his half smile, an eyebrow raised. I shake my head. He shrugs. He gets a drink. The first time he drank from the pitcher, it irritated me. His lips on *my* pitcher. This stranger. This forced intimacy. Then it became *the* pitcher. And now it doesn't matter anymore. He points to the drain. I turn my head to the wall. It makes him smile. I'm certainly not going to watch him take a piss. When he's done, he lets me know by touching my shoulder.

I get up to go for a run. I remove my skirt. I leave it on my mattress. I feel Julian's hand on my arm. My heart jumps. I manage to conceal it. I turn around. Moving the index and middle fingers of both hands, he mimes two people running together. I frown. I don't know. Run together. Why? How do I make him understand that I don't want to? I have no good reason to support my refusal. No way to make him understand. I accept with a quick nod of my head. He places himself to my right. We begin slowly. A fast walk. It's okay. Then I speed up. He follows behind. He passes me. Then slows down in the corner. I don't anticipate this and his elbow strikes me under the chin. It's like a punch right to the face. I stop. I see stars. He turns around. The point of impact is clear from my hands cradling my jaw. He comes towards me. I get ready for his anger. I should have slowed down. He comes even closer. His confusion is evident. On his lips, I read his apologies. He pulls my hands away and looks under my chin. His thumbs trace the line of my jawbone.

His eyebrows are so tense they merge into one. I try to make him understand that it's nothing, it'll be all right, but he isn't looking at me. He is so close that my hands are stuck between our two bodies. I keep my eyes fixed on the ceiling while he checks my chin. It appears everything is in one piece. He removes his hands and I lower my head. Okay. I'll let him run ahead of me. As I'm trying to make him understand, he seizes my face with his two hands, his eyes full of anger. For a fraction of a second, I think he's going to bite me. His nose is pressed against mine, he's not looking at me, he's too close. His eyes are fixed on my mouth. His thumbs gently separate my lips. I realize at the same moment that I'm bleeding. The taste of blood. The smell of blood. He pulls back to take in my whole face. He pulls on his tongue. I pull on my tongue. He lets go a sigh of relief. Even if I can't hear it, my brain registers the movement and imagines the sound so perfectly that I feel like I'm hearing it. I've bitten my tongue. Without stopping to ask, he runs his thumb over the wound to evaluate the damage. I try to pull back but go nowhere. My head is clamped between his hands. An iron grip. A warning. I stop moving. His thumb completes its voyage. Beneath the blood, I can taste the salt from his skin. He comes back to my eyes. He mouths, "You okay?" I swallow. I grimace. I test my tongue against the roof of my mouth. Painful. A little. I mouth, "Yes." He drops his hands. He backs up a little. There's blood on his thumb. He wipes it off on his jeans. He takes hold of my hand. He starts walking. I do the same. He matches his pace to mine. We do several laps walking with the same rhythm. Then we speed up a bit. He makes his strides a little shorter to follow me, I run a little faster to follow him. We find a balance. We do several laps. He lets go of my hand. We run. For a long time. When the smell of his sweat reaches me, I realize how completely empty this room has been. And now a smell. Human. Masculine. It's not even unpleasant.

I wake up. I go to the drain. I drink some water. I wait for him to wake up. He goes to the drain. He drinks some water. Then we run. Together. In sync. We stop. He smiles. For a brief moment, he seems free. I don't think he was ever able to rid himself of his thoughts before he landed in my room. Maybe he never tried. Too occupied with wanting to get out of here. Too angry. I can't hear myself breathe. I can't get used to it. I take huge breaths, to feel them, but I don't hear anything. He comes over to me and takes my hand. I no longer pull back when he touches me. He frequently writes on my arm or brushes me with his hand to get my attention. This time, he places my hand on his torso, and puts his hand over it. I frown. This contact is a little more delicate. He winks at me. I don't withdraw my hand. I can feel the beats. In the palm of my hand. His heart beating against his chest. Slowing down. It's a little like listening to your breathing resume its normal rhythm. I close my eyes. I let the beats transport me. For a second, I can hear. Not with my ears, but I don't realize this straight away. I open my eyes. I mouth, "Thank you." He gives me a sad smile. He lets my hand go and walks back to his mattress.

He spends a lot of time with his eyes closed, his forehead creased with worry. He hasn't given up. He keeps trying to find a solution. A way out. He did it once. The marks on his arm. I don't know what he did. I'd like to know, but how would he explain something that would take long sentences to be comprehensible? I should have asked him before. I imagine the gears of his brain behind his forehead. I imagine the noise they make. I think about who he was before. I imagine him as the head of something. Someone used to leading. Taking charge. Mr. Inquisitive. Mr. Anger. And that permanent crease in his brow. A lot of worries. Maybe he works in a suit. He must be something to see in a suit. All that punishing energy dressed in a tie. My boss wears a suit, but he's nothing impressive. Even with a tie. He's paunchy. A potbelly and a temperament to go with it. But he's not all that important. Nor imposing. The respect I showed him wasn't real. It didn't come naturally. It was an act. A kind of convention. Julian, even without a tie, commands respect.

I walk towards him. He doesn't hear me coming and I have to brush his arm to get him to open his eyes. I take his wrist and run my finger over the white lines. I mouth, "How?" He points a finger at the globe. Them? They did that to you? I mime a knife cutting his arms. He shakes his head. He gets up, pretends to pick up his mattress and launch it at the globe. He leans down to pick up the imaginary pieces of shattered glass and pretends to notch his forearms. The lines are not on his wrists. He wasn't trying to kill himself. He wanted to provoke them. Make them react. Shake things up. I nod my head. Understood. He comes back and sits down. I sit down beside him.

I've started other little roads on the wall. The scraping vibrates under my fingers. A little time goes by. I turn towards him. He's watching me. It's nothing strange. He's not scrutinizing me, not violating me. He looks worn, at least on the surface. He doesn't see me. He watches the movement. Entertainment.

I'm sitting on my mattress. I've brought it closer to the wall. So I can lean my back against it, too. Julian comes over to me. He takes my wrist. I think he wants to write something, but he pulls my knees up, folds my arm and rests it on my kneecaps. He sits down in front of me and places his fingers on my arm. Then he starts playing the piano. He plays the piano! My eyes open wide. He smiles. He stops. I mouth, "Again." He starts playing. I extend my arm to give him more playing surface. He shifts his position and continues. I can imagine the notes. I smile. He stops. He points at my smile. He gives me a thumbs-up. Then he goes back to playing imaginary notes for my deaf ears. I smile. I watch his fingers dance about. Then I see. I see it. I grab his hand. I spread his index and middle fingers apart. It's there. The tiny trace of an injection. I look up. He looks at it. He looks at me. There's nothing we can do.

I open my eyes. I say, "Do you hear me?" I can hear myself. From a distance. As if I were separated from my voice by three walls. But I can hear. I shout, I howl: "Julian!"

I push my voice so hard I can almost feel my throat ripping. He shifts in his sleep. He never shifts in his sleep. I run to his mattress. I shake him. He opens his eyes. I scream over the pain.

"Julian, do you hear me? I can hear myself!"

He leaps up as if I had electrocuted him. He takes me by the shoulders, pulls me up.

"Do you hear me? Tell me that you hear me! For Chrissake, tell me!"

His voice sounds even farther away than mine, but I hear him. He pulls me to him and hugs me with all his might. I explode in laughter.

"Your laugh! You're laughing, I can hear you. Oh, I can hear you!"

He starts laughing himself. His mouth is against my ear and I can hear him as well as I can feel him.

His laughter, I feel it, I hear it in my arms. It's an incredible sensation, exactly the same emotion at the same time. It's not words. It's a state. A sharing. A connection. I'm laughing, I'm happy. He's laughing, he's happy. That's it. One moment. One second.

I don't open my eyes. I'm listening to the sound of my breathing against my hand. I'm listening. The sound of wind. I miss the wind. I keep my eyes closed. The slight whistle in Julian's breathing. I can hear it. The soft squeak of the springs in my mattress as it follows the movements of my breathing. The almost imperceptible buzzing of the light. I didn't hear it before. I hear it. I can hear.

"Do you want to learn the waltz? I can dance the waltz. I can show you. It's something to do."

The waltz? We went for a run. I drew. He stared at the light. I'm on my mattress. He's on his. To dance. With imaginary music. No. I always say no to anything unfamiliar. Especially when the risk of ridicule is high. Then I look at Julian. No ridicule in sight. And it's something to do. Simple. Something you can't put a price on.

"I . . . okay."

He gives me a thumbs-up. He stands.

"I have a terrible voice. I can't sing, but I'll hum the tune. For the rhythm. You're not allowed to laugh at me."

He looks stern, but his eyes are smiling. He offers his hand. I place mine in it. He puts my arm on his shoulder. He's a head taller than me. He slips his arm around my back. He shows me the basic steps. I try to follow. It takes all my concentration. I'm looking at the floor. I'm looking at my feet. He lifts my chin.

I'm scared I'm going to step on his toes. Then I realize it's not true, I'm not afraid. We're both barefoot. I feel his movements, I feel the movement of air, I feel the heat from his feet. I'm not stepping on his toes. He straightens my shoulders. There are muscles in my back that have been sleeping their whole lives, and they wake up screaming. He adjusts my ribcage by pressing his fist into the small of my back. My muscles find their place. Their use. It creates a heat. I'm no longer a limp rag. It's exhausting. It's liberating. I like to dance. I had no idea. I like the waltz. It's not too fast. It's like skating on a cloud. He spins me around. I lose my balance. It doesn't matter. I start over. Again. I'm dancing. Well, he's dancing, and I'm following him. He guides my steps, he guides my movements, he guides me. He started by counting. Now he's humming. I don't find his voice unpleasant. Actually, it's so deep that I find it relaxing. I close my eyes. Just like when I'm running. I'm somewhere else. The movement rocks my thoughts like a cradle. They've gone to sleep and I'm dancing. Locked away in a jail cell. We're dancing. He stops. I open my eyes. There's something in his. Something that doesn't belong to me. A memory? I don't dare ask. The rumblings of anger. He is far away. Far from here. Far from me. I don't know what to do. I stand still. I give him room. I don't remove my hand from his. I don't remove my arm from his shoulder. I wait. He returns. Looks at me.

"That's enough for today."

I say nothing more. I will thank him another time. I don't know where he is. I think he needs to be alone. *That* I can give him. Solitude. He goes back to his mattress. He sits down, his back to the wall. Closes his eyes, tensing the worry muscle in his brow, and clenches his teeth. It makes hollows in his cheeks. His index and middle fingers roll the tiny invisible ball. I take a few sips of water, and I go lie down. I keep dancing in my head for a few more minutes, and then I fall asleep.

Julian is awake. He doesn't get up. He's lying on his back, staring up at the emptiness of the ceiling. I don't ask anything. I don't dare run. I don't dare draw. I don't dare disturb him. I don't know what to say. I don't know what to do. I say nothing. I do nothing. I am nothing.

I resurface. I was dreaming of sunshine. The sensation of sunlight on my skin. The heat. The intensity of colours under the midday sun. And the wind. The wind in my hair. The summer sun on my skin. I don't want to open my eyes. I want to remain in the sun. In the wind. The green. To see green. Trees. The blue of the sky. Before, in my life before, I didn't care about nature. When people invited me to go for a hike in the forest, I would say no. Too many mosquitoes. When they said I could sleep in a tent, I asked if it had air conditioning. I would say no thanks. The beach, too much sun. Too much sand. Nothing to do. Now. Now there is no more choice. Just grey. I resist for a moment. I hold on to the image of this invented summer day, and then I open my eyes. I open my eyes. No. I open my eyes. I can't see anything. Blackness. Absolute blackness. Julian. I scream, "JULIAN!" I can hear him moving. I try to calm down. Breathe. Julian?

"Julian, wake up."

He mutters something. I can't see him. I hear his breathing stop. Then speed up.

"Emma?"

"Blind. I can't see anything. You?"

"No."

Silence.

"I think they just turned the light off."

"Possible. I can't see the difference."

"There is no real difference."

The darkness takes up residence in my head. Acceptance. No panic. The deafness was temporary. The darkness will be too. It has to be. Breathe. Julian does the same. I can hear him controlling his breathing. His rage. His powerlessness. So much self-control. His voice is deeper than usual. More subdued.

"Are you okay?"

"I'll be all right."

If I'd been by myself, I would have panicked. I don't want to panic. I don't want to. I can control myself.

"What are they doing, Julian?"

I hear him take a deep breath. Control.

"We're lab rats. They're running tests. For what purpose, I don't know. Maybe it's the water. Maybe our reactions. That's the only thing I can think of."

I'd suspected as much. I hadn't articulated it, but I

knew it. In some remote region of my brain that I had blocked access to. In the same neighbourhood where I buried my fear. Singular. There are no more fears. They aren't distinct anymore. Just one big fear that embodies them all. Wrapped up in a shroud.

"Rats running round in a circle."

I can hear his half smile.

I get up to get myself some water. I place my feet on the cement with confidence. Even in the pitch darkness, I know the room by heart. I think I hear something break before I feel the pain. And the pain strikes. I scream. I hear Julian's reaction. He mustn't get up. I shout at him.

"Don't move!"

"Emma?"

His voice frightens me. It's what's in his voice that frightens me.

"I don't know what it is, but there's something on the floor, broken glass maybe. Everywhere. At least, I think so. I stepped right in it."

"Are you hurt?"

"Yes, I've cut myself. I can feel the blood running. Shit!"

"Are there still pieces of glass in your feet?"

"I'm trying…yes. Shit! They're too sharp. On all sides. I've cut my fingers."

I stick my fingers in my mouth. The taste of blood.

I run my tongue over the cuts. They're not big, but they're deep. Deep, clean cuts. I can hear Julian moving. My mouth is full of blood. I spit.

"Julian, don't touch the floor. Not even with your fingers. You'll cut yourself."

"I know. I'm using my T-shirt. It's everywhere. I'm coming, don't move."

The sound is strange. Movement. It's not the sound of broken glass. It's a sound I don't recognize. That I don't know. I can hear Julian muttering to himself. His anger. There is so much anger. It's an emotion that doesn't occur to me. Not to me. Anger. The conviction that what's happening to us is unjust. Undeserved. That should warrant anger. Why am I not angry? I feel sick. I think I need some water.

"Julian, the pitchers, I . . . I need some water."

I pull my shirt off. If it weren't dark, I'd be embarrassed. It's stupid. Julian starts speaking.

"Listen, use your mattress to move around. Get down on all fours, pull your knees up to your hands and push your hands forward. The mattress is pretty thin. It'll follow your movements. Like a caterpillar. Imagine a caterpillar. Head towards the pitchers."

I understand what he means. I put my shirt back on. I get down on all fours. I do my best caterpillar. I can smell blood. It hurts, but I can't stop myself from laughing. Maybe it's nerves. But I don't think so. I can hear Julian doing the caterpillar ahead of me. Then his voice.

"Do you see something that I don't?"

"The picture in my head."

I exhale. The effort. In the darkness, the sounds of our caterpillars breaking through a sea of glass consume everything.

"You there yet?"

I can feel resistance, the wall. I start to make a turn.

"I've reached the corner."

The sounds Julian was making stop. He's made it to the pitchers.

My mattress bumps into his. I can feel Julian's hand on my arm.

"You okay?"

"Have you got the water?"

"Don't move. I'm going to put the pitcher in your hand."

I feel his hand on my wrist, and then the cool pitcher against my fingers. I lift it to my lips.

"Sit down, stretch your legs out in front of you, towards me. I'm going to try to remove those vicious little things."

"Not with your bare hands."

"No, I'll use my T-shirt. It's already in shreds. Ready?"

As if I had a choice. Giving somebody a choice doesn't seem to come naturally to him.

"Yes."

I feel his hands touch my legs. He positions himself on top of them. He's heavy, but I know he's not putting all his weight on me. He places a hand on my right ankle. He has long fingers. They encircle my ankle. I can feel fabric brushing the sole of my foot. Gently. Stop at a shard, pull it out. It's not the pain that overwhelms me. It's the feeling of disgust. A foreign body scraping inside me. Inside my body. Julian manages to pull it out. I can feel it. Same feeling of disgust. Multiplied. I hear the fragment collide into others when Julian throws it to the other end of the room. One down. I feel the warmth of the blood as it flows down my heel. The fabric searches the sole of my foot. Another piece. Scraping. Scratching. Nausea. I try to breathe. Breathe. Think of something else. I can't.

"Julian. Talk to me, make me think of something else, otherwise I'm going to vomit."

The movements of his hand stop for a fraction of a second, then begin again.

"I don't like sausages. I hate them. Pork, beef, hot dogs, chicken, lamb, tofu. I hate them. It's not a question of the taste, it's a question of the texture. Or the image of them. When I was little, my mother told me that in the old days they were made with the entrails of animals. And ever since then, that's all I can see. My plate full of intestines. So, nope. No sausages for me. Never. Not even cut up. Never. And not even in the dark. I can't. I hate sausages. And don't try to psychoanalyze me, I'm not a homophobe."

He says it with so much conviction that I let a little chuckle escape. Julian doesn't eat sausages. He's not a homophobe. Duly noted.

"Vegetarian?"

"Oh no, not at all. Me man, me like meat. Just no intestines. And I have a fondness for cheese."

I hear a second fragment rejoin the multitude that must litter the floor. I take a deep breath.

"And this cupcake craze. You know what I'm talking about. Those little cakes drive me crazy. Chocolate is my favourite. In fact, I like everything chocolate. A real little girl. And I don't like the colour yellow. Not on walls, not on clothing, and particularly, not on my plate. My secretary says it's a guy thing. And I always counter by reminding her of my love for chocolate. And how I'm indifferent to pink."

He extracts another piece, which unleashes a nervous spasm in my leg. He braces my leg with his hand on my ankle. Firmly. My leg doesn't budge.

"You still okay?"

"Yes."

"It's better to get them all out now, otherwise the blood will coagulate and it'll be worse."

"Yes."

I can't manage to say anything else. I'm concentrating on Julian and his chocolate cupcakes without any yellow on top. The sound of another fragment hitting the floor. The cotton sweeps along my foot, then Julian's fingers against my skin.

"Nothing left on this side."

I hear him tear another strip off his T-shirt. He wraps my foot with it. He tightens the bandage. He pats it with his two hands. To check. Then his iron grip takes hold of my other ankle. There is silence. Then a big sigh.

"I was in my office. Past midnight. I often work late. They jumped me in the underground parking lot as I was walking to my car. Just like in the movies."

I remember the scene from my movie as well, while he extracts another fragment. A big one. I grind my teeth.

"They came up to me from behind and put a wad of gauze over my mouth. There were three of them. At least, I saw three of them before I lost consciousness. I woke up in a room identical to this one."

He tugs on a piece that doesn't want to yield. I hardly squeak, absorbed by his story. He continues.

"I thought they'd kidnapped me for money. So

in the beginning, I waited. I waited for a long time. Then it was too long, a ransom was unlikely. I got angry. I couldn't wait anymore. It was driving me crazy. To wait and not to know what was coming next. I started yelling my head off. I was more than angry, it was rage. I tried to break down the door. All that did was give me a sore shoulder. I stopped drinking their water to stay awake and confront them, but as long as I stayed awake, they didn't show up. It was at that point that I realized they were observing me. I tried to figure out how and with what. The globe was all there was. So I shattered the globe with my mattress. I thought I could smash the light and have the advantage of darkness whenever they decided to turn up. But the light is built into the ceiling, behind the camera. The globe is just there to hide their little toy. So I cut myself with a shard of broken glass to force them to react. They came. Three of them. I wanted to fight, to resist, but they showed up with weapons, one of them shot me. Just like that. A dart with a powerful sleeping drug. No confrontation. All they had to do was to step into the room and I was done for. I woke up on a thin foam mattress, all neat and tidy and back at square one."

Another shard lands to my left.

"And that didn't stop me! I poured the water out of the pitcher and hurled it at the new globe. It shattered.

Then I kept targeting the camera inside it. I managed to demolish the thing before they unloaded their sleeping dart. I went for another walk through wonderland. When I woke up, I was with you. And there you go. I think that's everything."

I feel him checking with his fingers. Then I feel the pressure of the bandage.

"Okay? Some water?"

"Yes. When was that?"

He places the pitcher in my hands.

"When what?"

"The night when they took you. The date."

"Oh, Friday night. June fourteenth."

I close my eyes. Even if it makes no difference at all. Almost two months after me.

"Almost two months after me."

Our first indicator of time. I take a few sips. My thoughts are scrambled.

"Stretch out and try to get some sleep."

I feel him get up from my mattress and move to his. I murmur a thank you. I wonder if they're going to put him back in the other room when the globe and the camera are repaired. I don't want that. I want to keep him now. I want to tell him, but I'm already asleep.

I think I've opened my eyes. There's still no difference. The pain is distant. As long as I don't move. As long as I don't walk. Unless it's pacing up and down on my mattress, that's not a problem. Julian isn't asleep. He breathes heavily when he's sleeping.

"Julian?"

"Hmm?"

"Where's the water?"

"To my left, wait."

I feel his hands groping around my legs, discerning my whereabouts in the dark. He leans a knee into my mattress and seeks out my arm, my hand. He places the pitcher in it.

"How do you feel?"

He's still on my mattress. His voice is extremely close.

"I'm okay, as long as I don't walk, I guess."

I pass the pitcher to him. He goes back to his mattress.

"I get the feeling we're entering phase two. The passive observation is over."

His voice is calm, poised. But he's holding a lot back. I wonder what would happen if whatever it is that's holding him back suddenly gives way. When he decides to stop restraining himself.

"What exactly are they observing? Testing what? And why us? Why you and me? And for how long? And how is it going to end?"

My voice cracks on the final question. The silence has time to deepen before Julian breaks in.

"If they take people, then it's to observe their behaviour. If you're asking me what the goal of the experiment is, I have no idea. But they've got resources. They're damn well equipped. And well organized."

I think about what he's just said. I can see images of military experiments. Just like in the movies. I wonder if I watch too many films if they're my only point of reference when reality is too much. I think about people who believe in God. Having a higher authority who exacts belief without rational explanation, that act of faith, seems strangely comforting. Perhaps. I'll think about the reality of a God when I understand why he allows so much shit to happen.

I try not to think about the fact that these types of experiments always end up badly for rats. In the end, if there is an end, they're not going to open the door for us with a 'Thank you for your participation.'

I can hear Julian's mattress doing the caterpillar.

He stops to my right. When he speaks, his head is at the same height as mine. He leans close to my ear. He whispers.

"I'm not going to just let things take their course. I'm not going to die here. I'm not going to let you die here either. I'm going to get us out of this rat cage, I promise you."

He squeezes my shoulder, as if to seal his promise. He moves back from my ear. I know that he's lying on his back, one arm under his head, like when he sleeps. I know he has no way of keeping his promise, I know he said it to reassure me, but it works. I believe him. I'm reassured. A little.

"Hey, Julian, how do I get to the drain?"

I don't even think about it, I just ask him the question. He's taken charge, something I never wanted. Something I'd never admit not wanting. I hear his half smile. I'm not imagining it. I know. I hear it.

"I emptied one pitcher into the other. We have a chamber pot now."

There you go.

Another day in the dark. I'm waiting for him to wake up. He's beside me now, on his mattress. I can smell his smell. The smell of his sleep. It's not the same when he's awake. His heat. His body temperature is higher than mine. And he breathes faster than me. He inhales and exhales in the same time it takes me just to inhale. His breathing changes. When he opens his eyes, he adjusts his jaw to make it crack. He's awake. He's going to ask me if I'm here.

"Are you here?"

Even in the impossible, even in the unbearable, there are markers of daily routine.

"I've been wondering what the point of an observational experiment is when you can't see the subjects. Why are they keeping us in total darkness?"

I hear him move. He comes closer, puts a hand on my shoulder. He doesn't even have to feel his way. He knows where I am. He puts his mouth next to my ear. He murmurs. He doesn't want them to hear us.

"I think they can see us, with an infrared camera

or something along those lines. I'm going to try something, tonight. I'm not going to drink any water today. I'm going to pretend to be asleep. It'll be my turn to watch them when they arrive while we're sleeping. Maybe I can learn something."

I turn my head in his direction. He senses my movement, and he shifts position as well, to give me his ear. I whisper.

"You're going to have to work on your breathing."

"What do you mean?"

"When you're sleeping, the rhythm of your breathing slows down. When you breathe in, it can last for up to eleven seconds, and up to nine seconds when you exhale. And you breathe from your diaphragm. But not when you're awake."

I can feel the surprise in his silence, before he speaks.

"Wow! Your ears make up for everything your eyes can't see."

Each one of his words smiles at me. He lowers his voice.

"I'll start training. Counting. How do you breathe from your diaphragm?"

"You fill your lungs until your belly sticks out. You'll recognize the muscles, the extra room your lungs can take up."

I hear him take a very deep breath. Hold it. Slow

down his breathing. I know he's counting. I count too.

"How do I know if I'm doing it right?"

There's no arrogance in his voice. I feel around a bit. He's lying on his back. I place my hand on his stomach. He breathes in. His stomach doesn't rise far enough. I place my other hand on his torso. I don't say anything, I wait for him to inhale again, and then I push down on his chest so he understands that his stomach must expand before his lungs do. He gives it several tries and then he gets it. He counts. He reaches his rhythm. It's pretty convincing.

"Is it okay like that?"

"Yes."

I hear him lift his arm and slide it under his head. Satisfied.

I want to remove the strips of cloth around my feet. They don't hurt anymore. I try to find the end of one of the bandages.

"Hold on, I'll do it."

It's like he can see in the dark. Julian shifts onto my mattress. I imagine him moving like a cat. The arch of his back. Crouched down. No longer any need to feel his way around. I might have superhuman hearing when my vision fails me, but he has the instincts of a cat. He puts his hands on mine. I pull mine away. He finds the knot. He undoes the bandage gently. The dried blood lifts off my skin with a sound that I

don't enjoy. He touches the wounds with the tips of his fingers. I pull my leg back abruptly.

"Does that hurt?"

"It tickles!"

"You're ticklish, huh? Let me see, I mean, touch to make sure everything is healed."

I give him back my foot. I bite my lip. I feel like laughing before he even puts a finger on my heel. He's very careful, but my leg keeps jerking away from him.

"I'm not doing it on purpose!"

He lets out a huge sigh.

"Put your leg down. I'll hold it."

His grip around my ankle. I don't budge. He completes his examination.

"Everything looks okay."

He switches to the other leg, immobilizes my ankle. I want to howl with laughter. He holds me down. The contrast between his grip on my ankle and the delicate touch of his fingers on the sole of my foot astonishes me.

"Perfect. No infection."

"Why do you think my feet didn't make them come but your arms did?"

"I don't know. Maybe because I acted like I was supposed to. There was nothing else they could do."

"Maybe because..."

"No."

It's a categorical no. There is no room for negotiation. And he doesn't even know what I was going to say. He doesn't give me enough time to explain myself.

"Don't even think about it. You're not going to cut yourself to see if they come."

He's thought about it, too. So it's not a completely crazy idea. He holds his tongue for a moment, and then speaks.

"It'd be pointless. You'd disappear for a while and then you'd be back with a few stitches extra."

"But if I injured myself seriously enough to require hospitalization? They'd have no choice, they'd have to get me out of here."

"That's only if their logic includes keeping you alive. Which might not be the case."

Not exactly nice to hear. I don't want to think about that too long. It appears they want to keep us alive, for now. But up to what point? And when? What could change things? What could tip the scales in the other direction? Do I really want to find out? I need to change the subject. Quickly.

"Are you a dad?"

"No."

"You have a certain paternal authority about you."

I hear him smiling.

"I don't have any kids. I have a little sister who I

took care of a lot. My mother was always working. Do you have family?"

"Only child. My parents had me quite late in life. They're retired now."

"They must be going crazy with worry."

"Not now, not right away. Not before Christmas. I don't see them very often. They live far away. Nobody knows that I vanished into thin air."

Julian doesn't respond. I don't know what to say. His silence weighs heavily on me. I'm looking but I can't find anything else to add. I hear his hand running through his hair.

"The night they grabbed me, I was getting ready to leave on sabbatical the next day. No contact with work for six months. I'd been planning it for a long time. Nobody's looking for me. No one needs to get a hold of me. Not for six months. My mother is dead. My sister, well, my little sister won't exactly keep trying if she can't find me. There's absolutely no one who knows that I've vanished into thin air."

There's a long silence. Then his voice, almost inaudible.

"They chose us."

They chose us. It's the first clear thought to come to me when I emerge from sleep. They. Chose. Us. I no longer open my eyes when I wake up. *I don't open my eyes.* I wonder how long it takes the body to adapt to a new reality. They chose us. I listen to Julian breathing in his sleep. Motionless. I wait for the handful of minutes that separate his waking from mine. I notice the dampness of my hair. I was groomed last night. A ball of disgust in my stomach. I can't do anything about it. They chose us. I begin to torture myself: Is it the men in black who are washing me? Shaving me? Do they make lewd comments? Say things about the state of my body? What else could they be doing to me while I'm unconscious? I can't venture into those possibilities. I grab hold of anything I can. A form of professionalism. Maybe my personal grooming is done by women. That would be less indecent. It's stupid, given the situation, but my mind hangs on to these details. Anchors itself. Otherwise, I start drifting. I can't drift off course. Not even a slight deviation. I won't come back. I know it. They chose us. They chose me. Because I'm insignificant enough to disappear without leaving a trace. Me. But Julian? How? Julian is taking his time to wake up. If he managed not to sleep, he saw them take me away. He's here. Nothing has changed. He did nothing. He couldn't do anything. Just watch. But he slept. He's sleeping. His breathing is more shallow. I feel like shaking him. I want to know. I don't move. I wait. They chose me. Me. Because I could disappear. Him too. I should cry. I should howl. I should. But no. It's objective information. Like knowing it's going to rain tomorrow. I can't change anything. Like the fact of wanting to move. Run. I'm sick of the limits of my mattress. I can't do anything. I've come to a standstill. I stretch. I sit down. I lie back down. I have nothing else to do. It's not enough. I want to get up. Run. It's an empty desire. Empty. Impossible. All I have are my thoughts. And I'm trying to avoid those above all else. Julian is waking up. Are you there?

"Are you there?"

He whispers. I get closer. I know that he doesn't want them to hear us. I lean my ear close to his mouth. His breath warms my ear.

. "I managed to hold on. I've never battled sleep so much in my life. They came. Three of them. They didn't turn the light on. All I saw was a faint glow in the corridor. It didn't cut through the darkness. They took you out. I couldn't see how. They didn't say a thing. They did everything in perfect silence. There was only the sound of boots on broken glass. Then the light in the corridor vanished. I didn't move. I continued breathing. You have no idea what it took not to attack them…I waited for the door to open again, but I couldn't make it. Their drugs have been in my system for too long. I fell asleep. I couldn't help it. You're here…"

There is something very tender in those last two words. I don't know what to do with all this information. I let my head fall on his chest. His skin. I'd forgotten that he didn't have his T-shirt anymore. I concentrate on my breathing. On his breathing. He runs his hand through my hair. They chose us. The bastards. Over my shirt, Julian traces the route of my tattoos, which run from the base of my neck to my left arm. They're black and visible through the white cotton. He noticed them. Before the darkness.

"Tell me, why the diamonds?"

My tattoos. Little diamonds. Big diamonds. Black.

"I wanted a tattoo. A dragon. On my shoulder. I was fifteen. My father didn't want to hear anything about it. He told me that if I got a tattoo, he wouldn't let me back in the house."

"The old man's pretty strict."

"Yes. Very authoritarian. Normally, it didn't bother me. But I really wanted a tattoo. I told him that if on my eighteenth birthday I still wanted one, he couldn't stop me. When I reached the age of majority, I went to get one. In those three years, dragons had invaded the shoulders of too many girls for me to still want one. I didn't know what to choose, so I opted for a diamond at the base of my neck. It was discreet. I could hide it under my hair."

"How did your father react?"

"He didn't speak to me for a month, but I continued to live under his roof. It was the first time I'd stood up to him."

"And the others?"

"The others?"

"The other tattoos."

"Oh, they came later, once on every birthday."

"Some are bigger than others, aren't they?"

"Yes, but for aesthetic reasons. It doesn't mean anything."

"And your father? He gave you the silent treatment every year?"

"No. He ignores them now. It's easier."

The family philosophy. Ignore the problem. They know that I drink too much. That I drank too much. But they acted as if that wasn't the case. They never spoke to me about my ridiculous job. As if I weren't wasting my potential there. If you don't talk about it, does it really exist?

"Well, I like your little defiant diamonds."

I smile. Mr. Business Leader. What type of business?

"Julian, what do you do for a living?"

"Oh. I run an independent firm that specializes in the global management of investment portfolios. Our long-term approach to asset management promotes stability and the attainment of our clients' financial objectives. That's our mission statement, word for word. Officially, we're portfolio managers. Unofficially, we're financial speculators."

I can hear his heart speeding up. I can feel the tension in his voice. He doesn't like his job. I don't like my job, but it doesn't put me in such a state. That was the only reason I kept it: it was a job that didn't put me in any state.

"Why?"

"Why what?"

"Why do you do that job?"

I can hear his forehead compressing. His jaw is tightening. His hand stops moving. Maybe I shouldn't press him for an answer.

"You know, I've never asked myself that question. I do it because it's extremely lucrative and I'm very good at it. I was eight years old when my father died. He was killed in a car accident. He had very good life insurance and it tripled because of his accidental death. He had left instructions for half to go to my mother, and the other half to go to me and my sister when we reached twenty-one. My mother still had to find a job. She had no qualifications. She got a job as a caregiver in an old-age home. She had a crazy schedule and lousy pay. She was a perfect example of what I didn't want to become in life. When I got access to my father's money, I invested it all in the stock market. I learned how to make my money make money. It came to me easily. I had a talent for it. Later I ran into two guys who did the same thing. We started a company and began advising people on their investments. I always went where there was money to be made. And that's why I do it."

"It doesn't seem like you enjoy it."

He thinks for a moment.

"I don't think you have to."

He's quiet for a while. A long while.

"That's why I decided to take a paid leave. I started to wonder how long I could go on doing a job that consumed my entire life and that I didn't like. Well, not really. I don't even know if the question is pertinent now."

Silence.

I'm dreaming of rain on my face. I can't remember ever being caught in the rain. But I'm dreaming about it. The rain and the sun. At the same time. The white light and the drops on my cheeks. I don't want to wake up. I don't open my eyes. But the darkness is brighter. I open my eyes and close them straight away. The light hurts. I hide behind my hands. The light. It's back again. I sit up. I open my hands. Slowly. I wait. I open my eyes, but keep my eyelids half-closed. I wait. I can look up if I squint. There's nothing on the floor. The room is the same as always. Empty. Grey. Julian. He's beside me. Our mattresses are beside each other. A little island in the middle of nowhere. I watch him sleep. I wonder if he's dreaming of rain. Colourful landscapes. Outside. Maybe he's dreaming of someone. A certain someone. Who isn't looking for him. No. Maybe he's not dreaming. He's starting to wake up. He doesn't open his eyes. I don't speak. Surprise.

"You're..."

He opens his eyes. Closes them. Hard. His face contorts.

"Ohhh! Light!"

"Yes. It's back."

I smile. I can see in his grimace the boy he used to be.

"Why?"

"The return of the light?"

He keeps his eyes half-shut.

"Yes, they take something away from us for a while, then they give it back. I don't get it. Is there something we're not seeing? Are we supposed to understand something? Come to a rational conclusion, a new behaviour? Is this behaviourism? Is this a punishment? Why? To make us lose our minds? What is it? WHAT DO YOU WANT FROM US?"

He hurls his words at the globe. Venom. He's trembling with it. I'm shaken by the speed with which he shifts from sleep to shouting at our prodigal sun with such intensity. I don't know if I could ever reach that level of fury, even if I practised for weeks. He turns his eyes to me. It appears that my expression speaks volumes. He looks confused.

"I don't know what to do anymore."

I get the feeling these are words this man doesn't pronounce very often.

"We could behave like good little rats and run around for a while. I really want to."

He gives me a contrite smirk and points to my feet. I show him the sole of my right foot. Before he touches the little pink scars, he stops himself. A smile, a real one.

"I won't tickle you, I promise. The other one."

I obey. He nods.

"Let's go!"

I put my feet down on the concrete. I wiggle my toes. I get up. My body is exultant. I'm moving. At last! Julian begins a set of stretching exercises. Stretching. Necessary. I can hear my muscles protesting. To run. I want to run! I start jumping up and down. Julian raises an eyebrow.

"Oh, isn't she the impatient one!"

And we're running. It's grand. It's good. To run. Who would've ever thought.

The smell of disinfectant. I can sense that my hair is damp before I even open my eyes. Then I smell something else. Blood. I open my eyes. I'm on my mattress. I take a deep breath. There's no way I could be wrong. Blood. Julian. I sit up. Something in my stomach rails against the movement. A groan escapes from my sealed lips. The blood. It's on me, under my skirt, on my thighs. Sticky. Almost dried. My period? I try to get up. I can't. The pain. I stay lying down. It's not menstrual pain. It's too sharp. Too precise. Like the puncture from a sword. My periods give me cramps, or they used to, when I had them, but it was a radiating pain, starting in my uterus and spreading up into my stomach in irregular waves. This is very different. I try see if I'm wounded, where the blood is coming from, if I'm still bleeding. It's difficult to sit up. I can't open my legs. I'm hunched up. The pain. I can't lean forward.

"Emma?"

His voice makes me jump.

"Are you okay?"

I don't have enough time to answer him. He's right beside me. Our mattresses are still side by side. When he sees the blood, his face turns white. Then he gets a grip on himself.

"You got your period?"

"No."

I wince. It hurts.

"It's not that, I ... I'm ... it hurts too much. I can't ..."

The raised eyebrow returns. His jaw tightens. He sees my damp hair. I can tell what he's thinking. What have they done? What have they done to me? While they were washing me. Men. An unconscious woman. His anger expands, his breathing rushes. His back straightens. I place a hand on his forearm. Stay with me.

"I can't ... look ... it hurts too much to bend."

My eyes implore him. I can't even conceive of the possibility of rape. I can't. Not now. It's too much. Just too much. I need help.

"Julian, I need help. I don't know where the blood is coming from, I can't see it."

My voice is strained, high-pitched. He closes his eyes. I count to five. He regains control. He opens his eyes.

"Okay. Can I?"

I nod. He positions himself between my legs. Kneeling. I'm lying on my back. I try to spread my legs. Slowly. I breathe. I feel his hands on my knees, on my thighs.

"Emma, I'm going to have to take your skirt off."

He undoes the button, the zipper, and then slides my skirt down to my feet. I concentrate on my breathing. The pain is tolerable. It's the fear of what it might be that's unbearable. He gets up. Comes back with the pitcher of water. He washes the blood off my thighs. The water is cold. His hands are warm. I try to concentrate on the difference in temperature. The feeling of water, the heat from his fingers. I can't. When I close my eyes, I see the men in black, I see myself, unconscious, sleeping. I see the worst possible. I try to tell myself that it's not true. It's not true.

"Emma?"

I open my eyes. He's above me. His face. I concentrate on his eyes. Green.

"I can't see any external wounds."

He's controlling his anger. He's used to controlling his anger. But he can't control the other emotion. The fear. He's afraid. For me. It's strange.

"Am I still bleeding?"

"No, but the blood on your panties comes from ... inside."

He doesn't avert his eyes. He stays where he is.

He's waiting. How far can I take this information? He's giving me the choice. To pretend. If that's what I want. He'll go along with it. With me. For me. Pretend. That's my first impulse. Act as if it weren't real. It's not real. I wasn't there. Just my body. If I don't think about it, it didn't happen. I could. But I don't want to. The look on his face. His face. The man who doesn't turn his eyes away. Who gives me the choice.

"Julian, I need to know. I want to know. The pain. It feels like there's an incision, a cut inside me. But I...it's not...I want to feel, check, but I can't, I...it hurts too much when I move."

I don't know how to say it. I realize what I'm asking as I formulate the question. The part of my brain that is desperately clinging to the reality of *before* keeps screaming at me that such things just aren't done. But *before* and *such things just aren't done* don't stand up. He doesn't even blink. He gets up, pours some water from the pitcher and rinses his hands. He positions himself in line with my pelvis. He kneels between my legs, bends my right knee and presses my thigh open. He holds my foot with his right hand. I close my eyes.

"Emma, look at me."

I open my eyes. His eyes are fixed on mine. He doesn't look at what he's doing. Respect. I can feel him moving the fabric of my panties aside. His fingers slowly spread my lips open. I can't help it. My whole body tenses. I grit my teeth. My back arches. The pain starts coming.

"Emma, breathe. If you tense up, I can't do anything."

I look at him. I can do it. I can. Breathe. I can feel his fingers, his finger, I'm not sure, entering me. Gently. It doesn't hurt. I breathe. It doesn't hurt. I keep my eyes fixed on his. It doesn't hurt.

"To the right. My right."

He puts pressure on the right wall of my vagina. He goes as deep as possible. I feel the rest of his hand pressing against me. Warmth. No pain. Then pain. A wave. Two waves. Contractions I can't control. The pain is amplified. He can feel it. He can see it.

"Emma."

His voice is so calm. How does he do it? I take a deep breath. His finger moves very slowly.

"Emma, I feel something. It's small. Pointed. I'm going to need my two fingers if I want to pull it out. Can you? Can I?"

Something? Something? What does he mean *something*? He's waiting for an answer.

"Yes."

It's a groan more than an answer. I'd like to be strong. I'd like to be calm. I would like to. He withdraws his finger. He holds my gaze. I can do it. In his eyes, I can do it. He inserts two fingers. I can feel the difference. He sinks into me. There's no contraction. I feel pain, but I breathe. Then he touches the *something*. A point of sharp pain. I wince but I don't contract my muscles.

"If this is what's making you bleed, I'm scared I'll hurt you even more by pulling it out."

"Julian, just get it out."

I close my eyes. I clench my fists. I breathe. He inserts his fingers even more deeply. His hand is almost completely inside me. Then I feel his fingers withdrawing. A warm liquid flowing. The pain is almost gone. Almost. I open my eyes. Julian is holding something between his fingers. He unbends my leg, then gets up. He comes to my right side. He helps me sit up. He opens his hand and shows me the something. An IUD. I have never had one. I meet his eyes.

"I've never had an IUD."

I take the little *T* covered in blood. I've never had an IUD.

"I've never had an IUD. Never had one. Never. I've never had an IUD."

I'm trying to understand. Why? I keep repeating it.

"I've never had an IUD."

It feels like I'm waiting for it to disappear. As if my words could somehow alter this reality. Them. They put an IUD inside me.

"They put an IUD inside me."

I keep staring at the intruder in the palm of my hand.

"An IUD ..."

His hand under my chin. He raises my head. I look in his eyes.

"Emma, is that the only thing that was causing you pain?"

Oh, all the things he's not asking me in that question. Everything it implies. A contraceptive device. It doesn't hurt anymore. It was the IUD, badly installed, that was hurting me.

"I think so. I think I'd feel something else otherwise. I think so."

And then it comes to me.

"It's a hormonal IUD."

I smile. Julian doesn't understand.

"That's what's preventing my period."

All the tension in my body releases. I'm smiling. Julian places his hand against my cheek. Comfort. He smiles too.

Another morning. I listen to him breathing. It calms me. I'm wondering if they put an IUD back in while I was sleeping. If they did, they did a good job. I don't feel any pain. It didn't hurt the first time they put it in either. At least, I don't think so. Maybe it did, but it was during the days with no water, and I didn't realize it. A question of priorities, I guess. An unauthorized surgical intervention. It's such an egregious violation of my rights that I should react. Protest. Get angry. But I can't. It's almost like I don't believe it. Like it was a dream. You don't get angry with a dream. You feel its effect on your mood for a few minutes after you wake up, but then you move on to other things, you move on to reality. But something remains. Something that's eating at me. I don't know. I can't put my finger on it. Julian. His breathing is getting faster. His jaw cracks.

"Are you here?"

It's no longer a question. He can see me. But I still like to hear him ask me. I turn towards him. He's staring at the ceiling, in his usual position, one arm under his head, the other resting on his stomach.

"How are you? Your stomach?"

"I slept like someone gave me a sleeping pill."

He smiles. He turns his head to me. He runs a hand over his cheeks. He's not shaven. If they came last night, it was for me.

"My stomach doesn't hurt anymore."

"Do you think they put in another IUD last night?"

I wonder if we think so much alike because we have so few distractions.

"I don't know. If that's the case, I hope they didn't put the same one back in."

I point to the floor. The one that Julian pulled out isn't there anymore.

"You shouldn't take this lightly."

His voice is cold. I can see the anger in his eyes as they return to their examination of the ceiling. He's angry not with me, but with the situation. But also a little with me. The one who doesn't get angry. Who doesn't react. Who says nothing. I make an effort.

"I'm not taking it lightly."

My voice is trembling. I try to control it, but I can't. That's why I prefer to say nothing. My voice always gives away too much. Julian turns to me. He's studying me. He says nothing. He's waiting for me to distill my thought. There's no thought to distill.

I'm not taking it lightly, but I don't know what *it* is.

"I'm not going to get angry at something that's beyond my control."

"That's not what I said."

His eyes are sombre.

"But that's what you do. You get angry."

"I'm not angry, Emma."

"But you are! Your eyes are screaming!"

He's looks at me as if I were telling him something new.

"I'm not angry with you."

"I wouldn't say just with me. But a little, all the same."

"What's wrong with you? I...I..."

He stops. He takes a deep breath. Control.

"I am not angry with you. I'm angry for you. Because you're not angry. Not enough."

Maybe.

I remain on my mattress, curled up in a ball. When Julian got up, he asked me if I was all right. I said yes. But that's not true. Not really. He didn't believe me. But he pretended to. He asked me if I wanted to run. I said no. He didn't insist. He doesn't insist. He glances at me from time to time. But he leaves me be. I don't want to run. I don't want to speak. I don't want to think. I'm tired. Not the fatigue that calls for sleep. The other type. The fatigue that numbs the machinery of the brain. I want to sleep. Even though I've just woken up. I want to sleep.

I open my eyes. It's dark. Shit. The light. Again. I stretch my arm out to touch Julian. I don't know if they've tried their broken glass routine again. I try to move my arm. I can't move my arm. I can't. I... can...not. I can't move it. I bump into something. Cold. I can't budge it. I want to sit up. I can't. I want to move my legs. I can't. I...breathe. I'm breathing. Maybe I'm dreaming. Breathe. Softly. I can move my hands. A little. My fingers. I feel around. A corner. I raise my head. I point my toes. I'm in a box. I think. I'm in a box. I'm in a box. I can't move. I'm in a box. That alarm...I've heard it before. Yes. The day I arrived. It's my voice. I'm screaming. That's it. I'm going to die. I'm already in a coffin. And I'm screaming. My throat is going to rip open. My lungs are going to explode. I feel my stomach contracting. No. A noise. Beneath my screaming. At my feet. A knock. On the box. I try to stop the screaming. It stops. I hear Julian. Far away.

Then not as far.

"Emma, you must calm down. Breathe. You have to hold on, stay with me, Emma, can you hear me?"

I want to answer him. I want to shout. My vocal cords are shot. All I emit is a faint squeak. I'm trembling. I can't control myself.

"Emma! Emma! Answer me, you can't give up, answer me! Please, Emma, answer me...Emma, Emma..."

His voice fades out with these last words. A continuous whisper. My name. I think that's what brings me back. Hearing that he can't make it without me. Him. I breathe. I knock against the wall with my index finger. A metallic sound.

"Emma?"

I knock once.

"Emma, they've stuffed you into a metal box. Those sons of bitches, I'm gonna kill them. I swear, I'm gonna rip the skin off their bones, I'm gonna... the bastards."

I hear him moving away.

"I'm gonna...I'm gonna..."

He's roaring. I can hear him yelling the most insane indignities. All directed at the globe. I concentrate on his anger. It allows me to stay calm. I can't think of myself. I can't inhabit this body. I project all my thoughts on to him. Julian and his anger. Julian when he's angry. Because of what they've done. To me. Julian who bawls and bellows. I think that whatever was holding him back has just given way. Full-scale anger. I hear water being poured on the floor. A pitcher. Glass shattering. The globe. His voice is so low, so menacing, that I can't make out what he's promising to put them through. I hear the pitcher striking the camera. Again. Again. Again. Then the noise as it crashes down. The camera. They're going to show up. Julian. He's in a trance. He's not even speaking words anymore, he's growling. They're going to kill him. No. Julian. I scream. Over my damaged vocal cords. Julian! Over the torn muscles in my throat. Julian, Julian, JULIAN! NO!

Then I hear him. In my right ear. Very close.

"Emma. I'm here. Can you hear me? Are you there? Are you there? Tell me that you're there."

I turn my head slightly to the right. I can see small air holes. Very small holes. Julian is on the other side. Julian. I wonder how someone can mean so much to me when I don't even know his last name. Is it important? I grumble an answer.

"Julian. I'm okay. I'm breathing. Please calm down, you're scaring me. They're going to come and get you. They're going to take you away. I won't be able to hang on if they come and get you. If something happens to you. Please."

My voice is a desert. Dry, grainy, with gusts of

wind that pass across it. I hear him sit down and lean against the box.

"I'm trying to unscrew the screws. There's nothing my fingers can grip onto. Wait a minute. My zipper."

I can hear him taking his pants off. I remember his underwear. I saw it the day they took away our hearing. Grey briefs. I can picture him. His long thighs. I close my eyes. I breathe. He's scraping the lid, an irritating squeak-squeak. It reverberates right down into the pit of my stomach. He mutters something and then swears.

"Julian?"

All I can do is whisper.

"I...It's nothing. It's not working, the metal tab is too big."

I hear him get up, walk. Noises. He's moving something around. The pieces from the camera. He's coming back.

"I think I've found something that might work."

I hear him working away at a screw. I have never felt so close to madness as I do now, locked inside this metal coffin. It feels like my heart is going to explode because of the pressure. Like all my organs have doubled in size and weight. There's not enough space in my body to contain them. It hurts everywhere. Internal pressure. I have to control my thoughts. Julian. In briefs.

"I'm getting there, Emma, but it's going to take a while. You can't give up. Stay with me. Are you there? Emma, are you listening to me? You're outside with me. Outside, okay? In a big field. A huge field. The sky is blue, the clouds are so high that it makes us both dizzy to look at them, there's a gentle wind, you know, a summer breeze, warm and lazy, just enough to lift your black hair. Okay? In a big field. Full of flowers. What are your favourite flowers, Emma? Tell me."

He speaks slowly, softly, but I can hear the physical effort beneath the control of his voice. I can hear the sound of metal striking metal. Something turning, squeaking, moving. Repetitive. I close my eyes. I can make it. I can see the field. I can see Julian in the sun. His green eyes sparkling. Daisies. I like daisies. I mumble.

"I like daisies. I like white flowers."

A sigh. Relief.

"So a field full of daisies. As far as the eye can see. Nothing but sun, wind, tall grass, and daisies. A ton of daisies. We're almost hidden from view, sitting on a big blanket. It has to be a red and white checkered tablecloth, you know, just like in the movies. We're having a picnic. Tell me what you want in our hamper. Whatever you like."

"Music? I miss music."

"Yup, music too. It's our paradise, everything you've ever wanted."

I can see it. In my head. Paradise. I can. Almost as clearly as if I were dreaming. I invest everything in this image. Everything that can take me far from here. The scent of flowers, the warmth of the sun on my skin, the wind in my hair, my toes in the grass, Julian's smile. I whisper.

"I want fresh bread and pâté. And cheese. Do you like cheese? I want grapes. And cantaloupe. Oh, and I want cinnamon buns! And café au lait, and little chocolate cakes..."

"Now you're talking! Do you see them? There are birds in the sky, and we're surrounded by butterflies. And music. What music?"

I think of him, Julian, his fingers playing my arm. A hundred years ago.

"Piano. *The Legend of 1900*, the music from the film."

My voice is nothing more than a murmur, but I don't stop. I concentrate in order to forget my body, to stay in my head. I'm not in a metal coffin. I'm in a field. With music in my ears. Cinnamon buns. Flowers. Julian.

"Yes, yes, I know it, Ennio Morricone. Never seen the film."

"It's fantastic, you'll see."

The squeaking stops for a moment. A fraction of a moment. Barely noticeable. But a pause nonetheless. Because of what I said. Get out of here. See a film. I said it without thinking. I have to believe that I believe it. That a part of my brain believes it. That I believe him, Julian. He's going to get us out of here. Confidence. In spite of myself. I don't want to waste anymore time here. Not now. Especially not now. Julian.

"It's a date."

The squeaking stops. I hear something bouncing off the floor.

"That's one."

A screw. Julian changes position and the squeaking starts again.

"Stay with me, okay? We're on the blanket, surrounded by flowers. Coffee, sugar?"

"Yes..."

I have to concentrate, to recall the taste of sugar in my coffee. The smell of coffee. The taste of coffee. The five coffees it takes me to recover from a night of tequila. Tequila. I didn't think to bring any to our picnic. Something has changed.

"Okay, good lookin', what do we do after the picnic? Don't tell me you want to run. We've done enough running around. We could waltz. We could swim. Do you like the water? Because I can put a big lake right there, in our field. A big lake full of clear water. Do you want to dive into the water? Emma?"

Water. Swimming. It's one of the only physical activities I've ever practised. Before. I like the water. The lightness of the body in water. The feeling that being underwater is like being in another world. I like the water.

"Yes."

My throat is too dry. A single word provokes a coughing fit. The echo rattles my coffin and alerts Julian.

"Emma? Emma, you okay? I'm going to stand you up. Why didn't I think of that before..."

I can feel the box shift. I can hear him breathing hard. Forcing it. I slide across the one centimetre of play I have and find myself on my feet. It's better. A little. The squeaking starts again.

"Okay, to the water! First one there! Go on, run, Emma! The water is cool. I can see you with your mischievous eyes. You're a much better swimmer than I am, aren't you? I bet you are. I try to catch you, but you keep slipping through my fingers. But I'll catch you, and I'm going to tickle you! Just you wait!"

I see him. I see myself running in the water. Throwing myself into the water. Weightlessness. The weight of a body that no longer exists. If you agree not to resist. I see Julian laughing. I hide beneath the water. The silence. I see Julian under water. His face distorted.

Bubbles rising to the surface. I can stay here a long time, always under water. It's a dream. I don't need to breathe. Julian catches hold of me. I'm not in any danger. He will never hurt me. Not him.

"And that makes two. I'll get there, Emma. Don't let go of me."

Me? Let go of him? He's doing all the work. He's holding me. I know he is. I feel it. I can hear him. From a distance. I'm in the water. I feel good. Julian gives me his half smile and bubbles stream out of his nose. The light from the sun pierces the water. Millions of tiny stars twinkle around us. He's laughing. I feel good. Then I feel tension. Something yanks me out of my reverie. I open my eyes. Blackness. Pain. My stomach. A sharp pain. A cramp. I can't bend over. I scream. It's not a scream. It's the growl of an animal. The squeaking stops.

"What's happening?"

I can't answer. I'm in a coffin. I'm here. Inside all the pain in my body. I am. Here. Panic has just broken through. It takes over. It wants out. I want out. I can't calm down. I want out. I want out. Out. I bang with my fists. I bang with my knees. I bang with my head. Forwards, backwards. My body stiffens. Convulses. I bang my head. I growl. I don't know who I am anymore. I'm an animal. I'm panting. I feel my body arc. Arc again. I'm not in control. I'm not in control.

I want out. Growl. I feel the box topple over. Then I feel nothing. I'm not here.

Hands under my armpits. Someone is pulling me. Something grates at my back. I'm not conscious. Not exactly. I can see the grey. I can see Julian. From a great distance. At the other end. Far away. My head tips over. I don't see him anymore. I have to climb back up. Towards the grey. Towards Julian. From the depths of the lake, I have to climb back up. I see it in his eyes. Worry. No. Dread. I must. I feel like I'm swimming in glue. My movements are slow. Too slow. I climb slowly. It takes all the energy I have left. Climb. I want to sleep. I mustn't. I have to climb. Or sleep. Die. Here. Distant. In glue. No. I can do it. I hear him. Julian. Shout. I can, I can, I...I open my eyes. Julian. He's asking if I'm here. There's water in his eyes. We were underwater. I say yes with my lips, I have no voice left. He puts his arms around me, hugs me, cradles me. He passes his hand through my hair. Something is pulling. Sticking. He puts his lips against my forehead. It still feels unreal. A dream. Am I here? Then I see the coffin. The metal box. A sardine can. Not even a quarter of the lid pried open. Folded back. Twisted. Destroyed. Covered in blood. My blood? His blood? I fall back into my reality. It doesn't make a sound, but I feel the shudder. I pull away. Julian opens his arms. I look at his face. He's aged ten years. His hands are covered in blood. His arms, too. He sees my eyes open wide. With fear.

"Julian?"

"I'm okay. Everything's okay. You stopped answering, there was no time left. I forced it open. I didn't notice the blood, I didn't feel anything. I wasn't careful enough when I pulled you out. I think I hurt you. Your back. I had to get you out of there. I'm sorry."

I look down. I'm covered in blood, his blood. My blood. I can feel warmth in my back. Scratches and scrapes. Cuts. Maybe. The coffin. I was in a fucking coffin. I was. I'm alive. I'm here. Julian got me out. I look up at him. He lifts his hand and wipes something from my cheek. I'm crying. Tears. They don't stop. A deluge of tears onto my cheeks. Onto my shirt. Tears that create darker blood stains on top of the blood that has begun to dry. There are no sobs. No wrenching of the head. Just tears falling like rain. Julian. I lean my forehead against his shoulder and I let the water flow. Little rivulets course down his bare torso until they meet his jeans. He says nothing. He puts his hand on my head and waits. He gives me time. Space. He's here. For me. The one who's crying. I'm crying. I can't stop myself. It lasts an eternity. It last two minutes.

There are no more tears. I raise my head. Julian tucks my hair back behind my ear.

"Can I take a look at your back?"

I nod. I look at his hands.

"I'm going to clean my hands, too. Emma, can I have your shirt? The cotton would be a lot softer than my jeans."

I try to pull off my shirt. It's difficult. I hurt everywhere. As if someone had beaten me with a baseball bat.

Julian helps me. He goes to get the pitcher that didn't take part in the attack on the globe and the camera. There's debris everywhere. A real mess. It's usually so empty. A false impression of order. Julian sidesteps the debris. He comes back with the pitcher. Passes it to me. I'd forgotten thirst. I take a few sips. I can feel the irritation in my throat. I keep drinking anyway. Julian pours water on my shirt, on a clean section. I murmur.

"You first."

He looks at me. Decides not to contest. My face must look more awful than his. He removes the blood. The white shirt takes on a reddish pink hue that makes me sick. Julian's blood. Because of me. No, oh no.

Because of them. The bastards. There's no more blood to hide his wounds. His hands are in a terrible state. Strips of flesh dangling. Julian plucks them off as if he were removing a glove. Without even quivering. A feeling that I don't recognize begins to ripple the muscles of my stomach. It doesn't hurt. It's more like a kind of weakness. Localized in my stomach. A tickling that is too intense to be enjoyable. And it happens every time Julian pulls off a piece of skin. It's as if I were feeling his pain. As if I were in pain for him. As if it were a part of me that was suffering.

"Come here. I want to see your back. If it's too painful, let me know."

I turn so he can see my back, but I don't feel anything. I can still feel the sensation in the pit of my stomach. A physical reaction produced by the simple act of seeing him in pain. What kind of connection can create that? Julian turns me around to face him. My shirt is no longer white. It's a reddish-brown ball on the floor. The pitcher is almost empty. He offers me the last few sips.

"They're not deep, but they cover almost the entire surface of your back. I should have been more gentle, but I had to get you out of there. You stopped answering."

I shake my head. He doesn't have the right to feel guilty. I get closer to his ear. I murmur, "Thank you."

He got me out of the coffin. That's all I need to know. There's nothing more to say.

"We'll get out of here. Just you wait and see. I'm going to get us out of here."

He gets up and extends his hand. I don't dare put my hand in his. I'm afraid of hurting him. I take his wrist. He gives me a sad little smile. We walk to the mattresses. He sits down with his back to the wall, his long legs stretched out in front of him. I lie on my side to leave my back free. I lean my head on his thighs. I close my eyes for a moment. I don't want to sleep. I'm scared that I'll wake up in the coffin. I'm fighting it. I'm exhausted. Julian absentmindedly strokes my hair with the back of his hand. Then, without realizing it, I fall asleep.

The sound of a door closing. I open my eyes. There's something near the door. I hear Julian breathing. He must have fallen asleep, too. No, his breathing is too slow, too light. I sit up. Too quickly. Dizzy. Then I see his face, too pale. And the blood. There's blood on the mattress. A lot of blood. Too much. It makes a path to the drain. One of the cuts on his left hand. My stomach cramps instantaneously. It knocks the wind out of me. Julian. He's bled too much.

"Julian? Wake up! Julian! JULIAN!"

He's mumbling. He doesn't open his eyes. He's still sitting. Against the wall. I place my ear against his chest. I listen to his heartbeat. I count. It's not beating fast enough. It's not beating strong enough. What am I doing? What are they doing? They're not going to just let him die, are they? I turn towards the door. I get up. I walk in spite of the dizziness. There's a cardboard box and a pitcher of water. I return to Julian with the box and the water. I open the box. I feel sick. A syringe. A syringe at the end of a tube connected to a needle. A blood transfusion kit. I close my eyes. I breathe. A needle. Julian. I can't let him go. I've seen worse than a needle. I try to talk myself through it. Since I've been here, I've known enough fear to drive anyone crazy. I've been more scared than I could have ever imagined. I can face a needle. A tiny little needle. I breathe. All right. Open your eyes. There's a sheet of paper in the box. The instructions. And a needle and thread. And a small bottle of iodine. And some gauze bandages. And some adhesive tape. The bastards. THE BASTARDS. I'm a universal donor. I know it. They must know it. I'm supposed to give him my blood. I'm supposed to do a blood transfusion. Me. And sew up his cut. Me. I can do it. I have to do it. I don't have a choice. I take a sip of water. It's not just water. A new taste. Medication. I carry it to Julian's lips.

"Drink, c'mon, drink. Please drink."

He opens his mouth slightly. He takes two sips. That's all. I shake him. He doesn't come back to me. I want him to be here. To help me. To reassure me. It's selfish. But it's better like this. He's not suffering.

I clean my hands with the iodine. I clean the wounds on his hand with the iodine. I can see the deep cut surrounded by mutilated flesh. It's still bleeding. My stomach does a somersault. I pick up the needle. My heart wants nothing to do with it. It's beating at full capacity. I try to forget that I have a morbid fear of needles. I try to think of Julian. His blood flowing. I thread the needle. I take a deep breath. I pinch the edges of the cut together.

"Julian, listen to me, I'm going to give you a few stitches. It's going to hurt. Stay still."

I push the needle into his skin. I run the thread through it. I want to scream. I can feel the thread chafing against his flesh and I feel like bawling. I make a knot in the thread. A double knot. I've done one stitch. I groan. Julian doesn't react at all. I tell myself that this is not a good sign. I can't think of that now. There are no scissors. I break the thread off with my teeth. I do a second stitch. I can make it. I clean off the blood, which is obscuring everything. I know how to sew. I sew up the wound. That's all. A third stitch. Maybe they're too close together. I don't want him to bleed anymore. I make it really tight. It creates a big fold of skin. He's going to have one nasty scar. He'll be alive. All right. Quickly. I do the other sutures more rapidly. Why did they not show up? They did before. Why not this time? Why me? I've finished. I clean up again with iodine. Then I pick up the syringe.

It's insane but the sight of the syringe petrifies me. I can't bend my fingers. I don't know what I'm more scared of—inserting the needle in my arm or in his. My stomach starts twisting at the thought of it. My hands start trembling. The last time a needle found its way into one of my veins, there were four nurses to hold me down and my eyes were clenched shut with such force that my face hurt for two hours afterwards. I can't close my eyes. I have to find my own vein. I have to do it. Stop thinking and do it. I run a bandage soaked in iodine across the hollow of my elbow. I extend Julian's arm and then my own. I take the tubing with the needles.

"Julian? I'm going to insert the needle now. I need you to be here. It's not going to hurt. Not you. But I need you to be here. Now. Julian. Please. Open your eyes, Julian."

My voice is trembling. Do I start with him or with me? The little piece of paper doesn't say. With him. If I faint, at least it'll be done. And if I miss the vein? If I screw up? If it doesn't work? No. Impossible. I can do it. I.

"Julian, here I go. You see, I'm picking up the needle. I can do it. I'm going to insert it right here, in this big blue vein, you'll see, it's not even going to hurt, you see? I've got it. I'm going to put this tape on, just like the nurses do in a hospital. It's done."

It's done. I did it. Nothing happens. I have to turn the little orange wheel at the base of the tube. I will insert mine first. The one for the donor. The chamber in the syringe is huge. Okay. I can do it. Think of nothing. Nothing. Nothing. Or howl. In my head.

To cover everything. Howl harder than anything. In my head. I push the needle into my arm. I scream at the top of my lungs. In my head. There's no blood. I didn't find the vein. I pull the needle out. The sensation makes me feel sick to my stomach. I howl harder. I pick up the tape and I make a makeshift tourniquet around my bicep. So I can see the vein better. My vein. I push the needle in a second time. Farther. Harder. I start retching. I stop howling. I swallow back the acid that has reached my mouth. Blood appears. Red. Dark. I did it. I turn the little orange discs at each end of the tubing, and my blood is on its way to Julian. I did it.

"Julian, I did it. I did it. Even with those fucking needles, I did it. You're going to get better."

I tape the needle to my arm with a piece of tape I've prepared. I think everything's going to be all right. I take hold of his hand. It's hardly bleeding at all. I can't believe it. I did it.

I sit down. I try to get Julian to drink something, but he doesn't react. I watch the blood travelling down the tube. I avoid looking at the needle. I'm waiting. I don't dare move. Then I look at the blood running between him and me. I look at the needle. Fuck my fear of needles. I can't do anything about the dizziness, but I can control myself enough to look at it, stuck into my arm. And in all this huge mess of intense emotion, I feel a certain pride. I can't even remember the last time I felt proud of myself. I get the feeling that this is neither the time nor the place. But I'm proud of being able to look at this needle. Happy that I can. That's it. I can. I take a deep breath. I stroke Julian's cheek, the way he so often strokes mine. It's been a while since they shaved him. His beard is soft.

"Julian?"

He doesn't react. Not yet. But it'll come. I know it. I feel it. I'm certain of it. I can't have done all that without it working. Then I realize the stupidity behind that thought.

I open my eyes. I dozed off. Sitting. I don't know for how long. Julian's breathing has improved. His face is not as pale. He's getting better. I'm starting to feel sick to my stomach again. I think I've given enough. I pull the needles out. I try to get him to drink. He doesn't respond. I drink. I put everything back in the box. Julian is still flopped against the wall. I lay him down on his back. I study his hands. His deep cut has stopped bleeding. I feel like shaking him. I feel like hearing his voice. I need to hear his voice. I should let him sleep.

I'm leaning against the wall. A stabbing pain reminds me of the condition of my back. I lie on my side. I watch him sleep. I can't do anything else. I don't have the strength. Maybe it's the transfusion. I'm not sure. There's no energy left in my head either. Exhaustion. Too many emotions. I don't want to sleep.

A noise. The door closes. I'm not sleeping. They came. And left. So quickly. I rush to the door. Shout at them. Talk to them. But I stop in front of the steel plate. It wouldn't amount to anything. Shouting. Screaming. What would be different today? Different from yesterday? From tomorrow? They left a small box. I open it. A syringe. Full. Something for Julian. I suppress a little chill. In front of the needle. Hardly at all. I pick up the syringe and head towards Julian who is sleeping. I'm not sure if it's sleep. But it has to be. Otherwise, I... otherwise, I don't know. It's sleep. I lean down, find the vein in his arm, insert the needle, and inject the liquid. Not even a single drop of sweat on my forehead. I put the syringe back in the cardboard box. I put the box back by the door. I walk to Julian. I lie down beside him.

I wake with a start. Julian. He moaned. In his sleep.
I sit up. I place my hand on his forehead. His skin is
cool. He doesn't have a fever. He's sleeping. Everything looks okay. But he's still sleeping. The little box
I put near the door is gone. I can't do anything more.
I look around me. Dried blood on the concrete floor.
The camera in pieces. The coffin. I drink. I go to the
drain. I drink again. I feel good. I decide to move
around a little. The state of the room bothers me. It's
ridiculous. I push the coffin next to the door. I pick up
the broken glass from the globe. I put it in the coffin.
I pick up the pieces of the camera. They join the rest
of the debris. The blood. Dry. I pick up the pitcher.
I wet the floor down. I scrub with my fingers. I pour
more water. It works its way to the drain. I manage
to clean it. To make the grey come back.

I can hear scraping. I open my eyes. Julian? The thought that he might no longer be here is unbearable. I sit up too quickly. Julian? He's in front of the wall with the little roads. He's scraping the concrete with something I can't make out. He's standing. He's awake. He's alive. I walk towards him. I stop. A huge sigh. Julian hears me and turns around.

"Hey, there you are. You okay?"

Me?

"Are *you* okay?"

"Me?"

"Yes."

"Why me?"

He doesn't remember anything.

"Er...you lost a lot of blood. You slept for a long time."

I take his hand. The suture is clean. No redness. No infection. It's healing. He looks at his hand. He runs a finger over the suture. Not even a little wince.

"Emma, are you all right?"

As if it were *me* who had spent hours flirting with death.

"Yes."

My *yes* is not convincing. I watch him as though he could disappear, right there, in front of me.

"And your back?"

There is still guilt in his voice.

"It stings."

I squirm a bit. I want to squeeze him in my arms. I don't do it. He's okay. He's awake. He's okay. He's speaking. He's speaking to me.

He turns his attention to the wall.

I move closer.

"I think the cement is just window dressing. I was studying your little roads while you were sleeping, and in one of the deeper tracks I noticed a difference in texture. Look at this. It's not a concrete wall. It's a layer of concrete over a wall made of plaster."

There's excitement in his voice. I don't understand.

"I don't understand."

"You can demolish plaster with a couple of good kicks."

I can my feel my eyes getting bigger. One more millimetre and they'll pop right out of my skull. A wall that can be knocked down with a few good kicks. A hole. To get out of this room. I look at Julian. He's smiling at me.

"First, we have to scrape off the concrete."

He shows me a piece of metal that comes from the demolished camera. I frown. His hand. It's not quite ready for this. I want him to stop. I don't want him to reopen that nasty cut. But I don't want him to stop. I wouldn't stop. Even with one less arm, I wouldn't stop. Why would it be any different for him? I say nothing.

I go to the coffin. I find a small piece of metal. It's smaller than the tab from my zipper. I look but I can't find anything bigger. I take my skirt off. I go back to Julian and I start scraping. Soon sheets of concrete are peeling off the plaster wall behind. It's becoming easier. The hole in the concrete is getting bigger. Julian goes to get one of the empty pitchers. He starts breaking down the plaster. The first blows don't seem to have an effect. He doesn't slow down. Banging. I'm so used to silence in the room that this noise seems right out of place. I tell myself that the din will bring them down here with their dart gun, but I don't linger on the thought. One thing at a time. Right now, it's Julian. Who is striking the wall. In spite of his hands. I get this strange sensation in the pit of my stomach when I look at his wounds, but I say nothing. I grit my teeth. I count the blows. A crack appears. Finally. Then an opening. Small. But an opening. An opening. A hole in the wall. Julian finally stops. He looks at me.

Never before have I felt inflated with so much hope. That's what I feel. Hope. Physically. Expanding inside me like a balloon. Making me light. Before I've even finished with the thought, my arms are around him. I hug him as hard as I can. He reciprocates. I back up with a smile. I put my skirt on. I get the other pitcher and I start demolishing the hole. There's room for two now. Demolish. With all my might. With all this hope itching and raring to leave. Demolish the wall with the blows from a water pitcher. There's a cloud of plaster dust around us. We're making an incredible racket. No one comes. Maybe there's no one left to come. I redouble my efforts. The hole is big enough to get your shoulders through. We stop. At the same time. We look. At first, it's impossible to see anything other than the cloud of white dust. Then the cloud settles. Another room. Empty. But it isn't grey. The walls aren't concrete. They were white already. There's no window. There is a door. Wooden. An ordinary wooden door. An exit.

Julian goes first. The hole isn't big enough to get his legs through. We don't take the time to make it bigger. He has to stick his head and shoulders through, and land on the other side with his hands, then pull his legs behind him. I try not to think of Julian's hands, which are supporting his weight on the other side. My stomach still does a backflip. Julian's feet disappear. It's my turn. I plunge through without a second thought for what I'm leaving behind.

Julian helps me up. My back hurts. I don't give a damn. We go straight to the door. I hear him hold his breath as he places his hand on the doorknob. It turns. He looks at me. I don't recognize the expression on his face. He opens the door. We enter a long corridor lit by hanging florescent lights. I can't see where it ends. There are doors at regular intervals on both sides. I feel like I'm in one of those endless high school hallways with their classrooms, but not exactly. There's no one here. There's no noise. Julian points to the right. We head to the right. We walk silently. The floor is cold beneath my bare feet. It's cold. But not to the point of freezing. It's just cold. There are no windows. Only wooden doors. Julian opens one at random. The room is empty, no light, no window. We walk a bit farther, and I open another door. Same thing. A dozen doors later, another corridor opens to the right. Just as long, more doors. Julian stops. Do we take the other corridor? I shrug. We head to the right. Julian opens a door now and again. The rooms are identical. We cross another corridor. It stops at a wall a few metres away. This is not working. The wall seems to have been stuck in the middle of the corridor. As if it had been built as an afterthought. To block an exit. The door on the right has a small window.

Behind it, some stairs. Which go up. We're probably in the basement. The stairs stop at the next floor. Same corridor. Same doors. Same empty rooms with no window. Same wall. This can't be the ground floor. Another juncture, same corridor, same rooms. My stomach contracts. The end of a corridor. A wall. Some stairs. To another floor. Same scenario. A basement with three floors? How many more? Hope suddenly bails out and leaves me with a sensation of vertigo. I can't think of a building whose function could explain such a maze of doors and corridors. Julian stops. He leans down to me and whispers in my ear.

"Something's not right. I don't think our escape is an escape."

That's exactly what my gut is shouting. The bastards!

"We're in a maze."

"That's the impression I get, too."

He opens the nearest door and enters. He looks for a light switch. It turns on a florescent light that sizzles before illuminating the empty room. No globe. No camera. I enter. I don't like it. The silence. The emptiness. The cold. The abandoned feel of it, contradicted only by the faint smell of disinfectant. The absence of dust. The emptiness. White.

"There's got to be a way out of here."

I can hear the anger rumbling beneath the calm

of his voice. He's holding it back. Staying in control. I'm starting to feel sleepy. I'm hungry. I'm thirsty. I'm cold. I'm shivering. I want to fight.

"Julian?"

He's studying the walls as if the answer were hidden somewhere in the white paint. I can't even remember which question I want him to answer. He turns his head towards me.

"Is it time?"

The concept of time has become so bizarre, but that's exactly what it is. The time when the drugs in our systems begin to take effect. The time for our night.

"I think I can hold out a little longer."

"Hold out only to find more corridors identical to this one? It's not worth it. We'll sleep here. I'll turn off the light and close the door. I didn't see a camera, they'll have trouble finding us. All right, come with me."

He takes my hand, we walk to the door, and he closes it gently and turns off the light. It sizzles for a moment and then darkness returns. Julian walks to a corner of the room, sits down. I can hardly stay upright.

"You're shivering. Snuggle up against me. It's the best way to keep warm."

I position myself between his legs, my raw back against his bare torso. All that separates us is the cotton of my bra. He wraps his arms around me. He's not warm, but he's warmer than me. It feels good. I lean my head back against his shoulder.

"Hold on for a second, I'll take my pants off. It'll be warmer."

He gets up. I stay on the floor. I hear him removing his jeans. He sits back down, pulls me against him, wraps his legs around mine and lays his pants over us like a blanket. He puts his arms back around me.

"Is that okay?"

I've stopped shivering.

He places his mouth next to my ear. Softly. His voice is a murmur.

"Thank you."

Thanks for what? My thoughts are tangled, confused. I wonder if I've known him long enough to sleep in his arms. I wonder what that means, *long enough*. I wonder if time passes when there are no road signs to mark it. I wonder if I'm going to be able to sleep, entwined in his limbs as I am now. I wonder what we're going to do tomorrow, even if tomorrow doesn't mean anything anymore, but I can't figure it out. I fall asleep.

I open my eyes in the dark. It takes me a moment to remember that I'm not in the grey room. I'm in Julian's arms. In the white room. In the maze. He's sleeping. He didn't move at all. His arms are still around me. His legs are still wrapped around mine. The tip of my nose is cold, but I'm warm. I have never slept in the arms of a man before. I could never do it. Regardless of the man who was sharing my bed, I couldn't do it. I would always wait for him to fall asleep and then I'd slide over to the other side of the bed. That was the only way I could sleep. I wonder if it's Julian who makes the difference or if it's the sleeping pill. Or the absence of a bed. His breathing. He's awake.

"You're here."

It's not a question.

"Julian, I'm thirsty."

"I know. Me too. Give me a little time to think."

I start to get up to give him his space, but he holds onto me.

"No. Stay."

I resume my position. I rest my head against his chest. He presses his cheek against the top of my head. His heart is beating against my back. He puts his arms back around me. I could feel penned in but I feel fine. Maybe it is Julian, after all. Then I hear it. He does too. His entire body tenses. The sound of someone closing a door. Far away. Julian puts his lips next to my ear.

"I think they're on the floor below us. C'mon."

I get up with him. I hear him put his jeans back on. We leave the room without making a sound. There's no one in the corridor. We run. With the same rhythm. Without a sound. Our feet strike the floor at the same time. We breathe at the same time. We take the corridor on the right. We arrive at a wall. A set of stairs. If it goes down, we're fucked. It goes up. Another corridor. An exact replica of the floor below. The three floors below. We start looking for another dead end to find another set of stairs. We run for a long time. Thirst makes running difficult. Fear makes running difficult. I try not to think. Just run. Just keep moving forward. Movement. We finally turn into a corridor that ends in a wall. The stairs go down. We're back to where we started. Julian turns to me.

"Are you okay?"

My throat is so dry that all I can do is groan.

"Let's go."

He goes first. I take a deep breath and follow him. I'm walking two steps behind him. I hear a door opening behind me. We both turn our heads at the same time. Three men dressed in black spill out into the corridor. One of them is armed. He aims his weapon at me. I hear the sound of a gun going off. He's shooting at me. I have no reflex. I keep walking and looking over my shoulder at the bullet that's coming my way. It's Julian who pulls me out of its path by slamming me up against the wall. It's Julian who takes the bullet in his stomach. It's Julian who collapses. I hear myself screaming. But it's not really me who's screaming. It's a woman I don't know. A woman who started screaming and crying and who collapsed against Julian's body, which had stopped moving. She howls at the moon. She screams with a voice that is no longer her own. She hurls insults at the men in black, but her words are meaningless. One of the men who isn't holding a weapon tries to lift her up. She refuses to move. He puts his hands on her shoulders. She punches him in the eye. She is in a state of rage. All the anger she has never shown erupts at the same time, all at once. Anger that multiplies the potential for violence, which erases reason. She is consumed by it. She is in an impossible state of distress. They killed Julian. Julian. He is dead. For her. She who is nothing. She bites the arm of the man who is trying to restrain her fists.

She spits out the piece of flesh she has just chewed off, accompanied by a trace of black fabric. The man screams and delivers a blow with the butt of his gun. On the head. She falls to her knees. She recognizes the pain, but she doesn't feel it. Not really. The pain is too small compared to the pain of seeing Julian dead. She falls. She gets up. She's not going to stop. Not this time. She wants to kill them. One of the men puts a cloth over her nose. She doesn't want to breathe in. She starts kicking them. She hears the weapon. The gun shot. Between screams, she hears the bang. Shot in the stomach. She falls. She sees the nape of Julian's neck. She sees nothing more. She's not here. It's not me. It's a young girl who's lost her mind. Who has lost everything.

My head hurts. I haven't opened my eyes yet. It's the headache that wakes me. Julian. JULIAN. I sit up as I open eyes. Another grey room. Concrete. White globe. Mattress. Pitchers. No Julian. They've killed Julian. He wasn't the experiment. It was me. They've killed Julian. The smell of disinfectant. I'm clean. I'm wearing a new white shirt. It's not dirty. It's not torn. I don't care. I'm thirsty. I don't care. They won't win. They won't get me. They won't get anything more from me. I have nothing left. I don't have Julian. They can go fuck themselves. I get up and launch the two pitchers at the door. I leave the globe in one piece. I want them to see the failure of their experiment. I want to see them show up and force me to drink. I curl up in a ball on the mattress. I close my eyes. The pulse in my head is throbbing against my temples. Hard. It's nothing in comparison to the pain that's ripping up my stomach. I count the beats. I count so I don't think about Julian. I count backwards towards death.

I sleep. I wake up. I don't really sleep. I know this state. The pain of thirst. My mixed-up mind. I let it come. It'll go quickly. Already more than two days without water. I think. When I sleep, I don't dream. When I don't sleep, I count backwards. When I forget where I am, I start over. Hunger is tearing at my stomach. But it's a miniscule pain. A bearable burning. Then there's the other pain. When I think of Julian. It doubles me over. I wake up whispering his name. I don't sleep and I whisper his name. I can hear him breathing, but he's not here. My lips are so dry that they crack and bleed. I have the taste of blood in my mouth. It's nothing. I count backwards. I lose consciousness.

There's a white glow enveloping everything. Even the men dressed in black. Them. Enveloped in a shining white fog. They're lifting me. They're taking me out. They're talking. I can't understand what they're saying. I'm flying. I think I am. I'm swimming. Yes. I'm in the water. It's the lake. Julian's lake. Where we had our picnic. With the daisies. Julian is in the water. His green eyes are shining in the sunlight. He's alive. I swim towards him. I'm happy. Are you there? I'm here. I've stopped counting backwards. It's over.

I open my eyes. I'm not dead. Julian is dead. I'm in the grey room. On a mattress. My head doesn't hurt. There's something new. A drip feed. In my arm. They've rehydrated me. They've fed me. The bastards. I don't want it. I don't want anything anymore. I yank the tube out of my arm. I go back to sleep.

I'm staring at the ceiling. The grey faux concrete. I'm going to live. They put the drip back in. I didn't pull it out. I don't know why. I don't understand. Me. Alive. Until when? For how long? There's something scratching at the edge of my consciousness. Something insistent. But I don't want to think. I want to forget. I want to stop hurting. It's not physical. My back doesn't hurt anymore. My head doesn't hurt anymore. It's what's inside me that isn't right. The feeling that the most important parts are missing. The most vital. It's the holes that hurt. I try not to think about Julian. But how do I not think of him? I don't have the strength to impose a direction on my thoughts, and all of them turn towards Julian. They shot him in the stomach. He's not here anymore. I'm still here. In the same place. In the grey. Useless. Nothing has changed. Nothing ever changes. Not here.

There is information at the edge of my fog. Something that is trying to give me hope. I don't dare. Hope seems somehow inappropriate. As if I were thumbing my nose at Julian. I go back to sleep.

I decided to get up. I couldn't take lying down any-more. I stretch a little. I drink from the pitcher. Auto-matic gestures. It makes me think of my life before. The one where I had a place of my own, a job. The one where all my gestures were automatic. Between my life before, in a cardboard box, and my life now, in a grey room, I wonder if there's really any difference.

The sound of a gunshot. In my dream. That's what wrenches me back to reality. I don't remember what happened after I saw Julian fall. I think I lost con-sciousness. But it's coming back to me, bit by bit. The taste of blood in my mouth. I bit the man who wanted to pull me away. I screamed. They hit me. I fell. It's the second bang that doesn't make any sense. That's what haunts my empty dreams. I don't know why. They didn't kill Julian twice. I don't want to think about it. It makes me sick.

Julian falls. The white corridor. The florescent lights. I'm screaming. I know it's a dream. I don't want to relive this moment. I want to wake up. I want to open my eyes. I can't. I'm caught in this dream. The bastards are running after me. I'm going to bite one of them. Spit out a piece of him. I'm going to be hit over the head. I'm going to fall. Pass out. But I don't pass out. The cloth over my mouth. I hear the second gunshot. Close. The light explodes. The dream begins again. An endless loop. Julian falls. I scream. They run after me. I bite. I spit. I get hit over the head. I fall. The cloth over my mouth. I hear the second bang. And it starts again. Until I finally wake up.

My face is covered in sweat. My muscles are tense, strained. I get up. I drink. I go to the drain. I piss. I walk. I've stopped running. I walk around in circles. I wonder if this is the same room where Julian was held before they placed him in my life. Everything is the same. The mattress, the globe, the pitchers, the door, the faux concrete. The same. I have no way of knowing if the room faces the same direction. It's not that important. I don't feel like drawing. I don't feel like anything.

The gunshot still reverberates in my head. The gunshot. The second one. I stop walking. I run my hand over the base of my stomach. The second gunshot. It was for me. In my stomach. Not a bullet, a dart. A sleeping dart.

And Julian? My body reacts. My heart reacts. And if Julian...? The thought refuses to form. If Julian isn't dead. I ransack my memory. Was there blood? Did I see him with his eyes open? Were they vacant? He fell onto his stomach. I didn't see any blood. His head was turned towards the wall. I didn't see his eyes. There was only one weapon. The second shot came from the same gun. It didn't kill me. It put me to sleep. Julian isn't dead. Why did they take him away from me? Where is he? I turn towards the door. I can feel my anger mounting. Powerful. I don't want to scream. I don't want to go crazy. But I don't have enough strength to stop madness from swallowing me up. I grit my teeth. Hard. My jaw cracks. I can feel my ears turning red. My hands are white. They're shaking. But I haven't lost control. I breathe. I breathe. I walk to the globe. I lift my head. My jaw is still clenched. My voice feels like it's coming from somewhere else. From every direction. Strong. Controlled. I point my finger at the globe.

"I...will...find...him."

I breathe deeply. I add one more word. Only one.

"Bastards."

I'm lying on my mattress. Julian. Even before I open my eyes. I'm not completely awake. The space in between. I didn't have the dream. Julian isn't dead. Maybe they've brought him back to me. I listen for signs of his breathing. But I don't hear anything. I try to remain calm. I have to think. There's another grey room. With Julian in it. I have to get out of here. We did it once. I can do it again. Find him. Find him again. I can't be alone. I put up with it before. But I can't go back to before. Between before and now stands Julian. I can't pretend that Julian doesn't exist. As if he never existed. I can't deconstruct my reality. Even if I could. I don't want to. I don't even want to try.

The wall. First I have to remove the layer of faux concrete. I take my skirt off, I get up quietly, I take the metal tab and head to the wall on the left, just like in the other room, that's if I'm facing the same direction. I think so. But that doesn't really matter. All there has to be is another room next to this one.

I start drawing. But I'm not drawing. I'm making a hole in the concrete. For them, I'm drawing. I start with a small circle, and then I make a spiral around the circle. A variation on my little roads. The ones I made on the other wall, in the other room. The ones that made me so happy, for a brief moment. But this isn't a road. It's a target. And I'm not happy. I scrape gently, so as not to alert them. I could destroy the globe and the camera the way Julian did. A piece of metal from the camera would be more effective than trying to scrape off the concrete with this tab. But I'm scared I won't be fast enough to break through the wall by myself. As soon as I destroyed the camera, they'd be on me straight away. And that wouldn't be good. So I pretend. I draw. I'm a nice girl. A docile rat. I drink some water. I walk. I've stopped running. I go back to drawing. My target grows. It's taking a long time. I dig deeper. All the way to the plaster. My fingers hurt. I keep going.

I think of Julian. In another room. Julian waking up, realizing that I'm not there. Julian who promised to get me out of here. Julian who doesn't quit, who never quits. What have they done to him to hold him down? Did they tie him up? Did they feed him sedatives? Did they eliminate him? I don't want to think about it. I can't think about it. My stomach is in knots. The strange cramp that I felt when I looked at his injured hands comes back when I imagine his pain. The sound. The sound of the metal tab against the concrete. I concentrate on the sound. I keep digging. The movement is repetitive, hypnotic. I slow my breathing. I listen to the sound. I focus on the movement of my hands. I'm almost in a trance. I don't even feel the pain in my fingers anymore. I dig. I scrape the concrete. That's all I am. Here. In this moment. A rat scraping its way out of its cage. Methodically. Relentlessly. I dig. I scrape. I don't stop.

I open my eyes. I take a deep breath in. I shouldn't rush to the wall as soon as I wake up. They could suspect something. Maybe they already suspect something. As long as they don't intervene, I don't give a damn. I get up. I drink. I go to the drain. My fingers hurt. My shoulders ache. There's a shooting pain in my lower back. I walk around a bit. I take off my skirt and go to the wall. One more day and I'll have a hole big enough to get my shoulders through. I'll be able to break through the plaster with the pitcher and go find Julian.

Today I don't open my eyes right away. I'm wondering if I should break the camera before breaking down the wall. I wonder if it's worth it. I get the distinct impression that their observation post is a long way from here. That I'll have enough time to get lost in their labyrinth of corridors before they show up. If they show up. I think I'll break down the plaster. I open my eyes. Yes. Drink, empty the pitcher, and break down the plaster. I get up. My muscles still ache, but the pain is less present. Less intense. I walk towards the pitchers. Something's not right. Even before I see them up close, I get it. They've replaced the plastic pitchers with containers made of Styrofoam. Which will crumble at the slightest impact. I stay still. There's too much movement going on in my head, in my body. All my senses reject this simple reality. No. It's impossible. It can't be. I look around. I'm looking for something. Another option. Another solution. There's nothing. Just emptiness. This fucking emptiness. I go back to my mattress. I lie down. I close my eyes. I'm not moving anymore.

I open my eyes. Darkness. The trick with light again. I let go a *fuck you*. I can't hear myself. I recognize the excess of silence. The pressure of nothingness. The trick with the hearing again. They can close up my ears. And what else? Not even the first signs of panic. My breathing hasn't sped up. I'm not pretending that I'm not afraid. I'm not afraid. I don't give a damn. I don't give a shit. The only thing I want is Julian. But they took him away from me. They came and took him away from me. They made me think he was dead. The bastards. Slowly I reach my hand out from the mattress. All I can feel is cold cement. Nothing sharp. I feel my way around the mattress. Nothing. I get up. I know how to do this without my eyes. I know how to do this without my ears. I know he is alive. Somewhere. In another fucking grey room. I know I can find him. Knock the walls down. I can do it. Even if it takes me ten years. Even if they sent him to the other end of the earth. I'm going to find him. I breathe. And then I feel him.

Everything in me freezes. He's not at the other end of
the earth. He's somewhere in this room. A few steps
away. I recognize his smell. It's him. He's here. They
didn't take away my sense of smell. I smell him. He's
sleeping. It's his smell when he's sleeping. All I've got
to do is find him. Before he wakes and starts moving.
I breathe in deeply. I'm shaking. My legs can barely
support me. I sweep my foot around in a semicircle to
cover the largest possible area. I take a step. If I listen
to my body, I'll sense the heat he gives off before I
find his mattress. They can't take away what I feel. I
comb the darkness, I listen to my nose, I concentrate
on temperature. A semicircle. A step. I don't think.
I'm in motion. I move towards him. A semicircle. A
step. I speed up. The cement is cool under my feet. As
usual. I take another step. Another semicircle with the
tips of my toes. All my attention rests in the few centimetres of skin at the end of my foot. I'm seeking heat.
He gives off heat. Especially when he sleeps. Another
step, and then I feel the slight change in temperature.
He's here. His smell hits me first, more intense, then
his body heat, and then my foot strikes his mattress.
Julian. At last. I kneel down, feel around a bit, then
I meet his shoulder. I place my hands on his chest.
Inhale. Nine seconds. Exhale. Seven seconds. I align
my breathing with his without even realizing it. A
moment of complete calm. He's here. His breathing is

normal. His smell is normal. I run my hand through his hair, over his cheek. He's unshaven. He's starting to wake up. I find his hand. I run my fingers over his palm. I feel his skin, rough but healed. I find the scar left behind by my handiwork. I leave my other hand on his heart. They've given him a T-shirt. He starts breathing more rapidly. His jaw cracks, sending a tremor down his whole body. Under my hand, I feel his heartbeat getting faster. Waking up. The realization of darkness first. I feel the vibration beneath my fingers when he tries to speak. Then his hands seek out mine. One hand follows my left arm, up to my face. He glides his fingers over the bridge of my nose, over my hair. He knows. He recognizes me. We're blind. We're deaf. We're here. He sits up and pulls me to him. He holds me in his arms. He looked for me. I know it. I feel it.

He takes my right hand. He makes room for me on his mattress. He holds me to him and hugs me tightly. He's not going to let me go. There are no words, but I hear what he says—he will never let me go again. He wraps his arm around me. His hand rests on my back. Absentmindedly, he traces the map of my tattoos. His breathing is regular. When he breathes out, it tickles the top of my head. There's nothing we can say. I don't even think. He's alive. I'm in his arms. I can smell his smell. His warmth envelops me. I place my hands on his chest and I feel his heart beating. For a moment, his hand stops on my back. He's here. With me. His hand climbs back up to my hair. Runs along the length of my face. Stops at my cheek. His thumb finds my lips. It passes gently along my smile. Because I'm smiling. His hand slides down to my chin and lifts my head, as if he wanted to meet my eyes. His lips touch mine. As lightly as a breath of wind. A kiss. Soft. Simple. A contact. In the silence, in the darkness, there's nothing other than my lips and his lips. And this kiss.

He hugs me. He lies back down and makes me follow him. His arms, his legs, he wraps himself around me. Then he stops moving. I stay like this, in the middle of him, pressed against his torso. My head on his arm. I feel his heart beating. I feel the weight of his leg on mine, the weight of his other arm on my hip. His hand in the hollow of my back. I let the hours of my nightmare slip far away from consciousness. Julian. Here. With me. We stay like this for a long time, without moving. As if even a tiny movement might change something about this state of serenity, as if moving might alter our reality.

I'm woken by fingertips. The darkness. The silence. In the arms of Julian. Julian's hand on my thigh. It hesitates. Like a question. He woke up before me. His hand stops at the hem of my skirt. I am still pressed up against his torso. I haven't moved since I fell asleep. I lift my head a little and deposit my lips in the hollow at the base of his throat. I can feel his pulse quickening beneath my kiss. His hand climbs under my skirt, up my thigh, very slowly, very gently. I don't hear the sound of the fabric crumpling. I don't hear the sliding of his hand on my skin. I feel it. His hand continues upwards, and then he pulls me even closer to him. I fit right into his body. I'm enveloped. By him. He hugs me. Gently. I'm not going anywhere. I'm here. Now. With him. He runs his free hand under my shirt to my back and draws the tips of his fingers across it. I know he's checking to see if it has healed. My back is healed. There's a pause. He hesitates. I squirm a little and I remove my shirt. I weave my hand towards his stomach to find the edge of his T-shirt and skim my fingers along his skin as I pull it up. He pulls the T-shirt off. I feel his body against mine, his skin against my skin. He flips me onto my back. Silence. Blackness. Each movement is slowed down, our bodies listening for what our ears can't hear. He presses against me. From the imbalance in his weight, I can tell that he's leaning on his right elbow. His face is right next to mine, a few centimetres away. His breath is hot against my cheek. He rests his lips on my forehead and then they drop to mine. The lightness of touch, floating, mercurial. I cup his face between my hands, and the stubble of his beard tickles my fingertips. His beard. His cheeks. Julian. I follow the line of his jaw with my thumbs, I drop down to his throat, I place my hands on his chest, I listen to his heart with my fingers, I listen to his breathing. I explore his stomach with the back of my right hand, leaving my other hand on his heart. I can feel goosebumps forming on his skin. I breathe in. My hands return to his face. I grip it firmly and run my tongue along his lower lip. I feel the sudden rush of air he expels against my mouth. His hand finds my chin, his tongue finds my tongue. His entire body weighs down on me. I feel his stomach tightening. I can feel his erection against my lower abdomen. My body responds before I know what's happening—my back arches and my pelvis presses harder into him. He slides his hand under my back. He guides my hips towards him. Our lips no longer need the help of our hands to locate each other. He opens my mouth with his tongue. I want him. Badly. My desire is so intense it's almost painful. Almost. His hand slides up to my hip, finds the route to my stomach and then to my chest. He slides his fingers under my camisole, lifts the elastic over my breasts. His lips pull away from mine, he uses his two hands to remove this scrap of cotton that I haven't taken off since I've been here. The air on my nipples is like a caress. Then comes the warmth of his hands. He traces the outline of my breasts—he sees them with his fingers, he imagines with his lips. When he draws his tongue back, the influx of cold air pulls a moan out of me that neither of us can hear. I don't want to feel his jeans against my thighs anymore. My hands drop to his hips. His hands take over from mine. He undoes his pants. I wait. He slides my skirt off my legs. He knows that he doesn't have to undo the button. He places his lips at the edge of my panties. An electrical current shoots through my stomach. I feel his fingers pry under the fabric. I hold my breath as they move between my lips. He discovers to what degree my body responds to his touch. There is an eternity when nothing moves, and then his fingers slip into the search for my clitoris. I try to remain still, but I can't, my hips begin to swing like a pendulum as they press against his hand, against his fingers. I feel him move between my legs. He withdraws his fingers to pull off my panties. He lies down against me. I insert my hand between his body and mine. I find his stomach, then his penis. I feel what I can't see. I enclose the base with my right hand, trace the fingers of my other hand upwards to the tip. The rhythm of his breathing quickens against my neck. His teeth sink into my shoulder. I guide him to me and he enters me gently. Slowly. A single beat. A cadence that allows everything to be felt. Everything I don't see. Everything I don't hear. Another beat. His lips. My mouth. The vibration of his voice. The beats of his heart. The penetration. The smells of lubrication, his sex. The blend of our perfumes. I straddle his hips, he digs deeper. He holds me, his hands cupping my face. I don't know where I start, I don't know where he ends. It's dark, there isn't a sound. And yet I hear him when he comes. And I know that he hears me, too.

I hear a noise. I can hear. I don't open my eyes straight away. Then I realize that it's not a usual sound. I open my eyes. I can see. The light is dim. But I can see. I see the tip of a blade of grass. I'm dreaming. I breathe in. I can smell it. Outside. I'm dreaming. I close my eyes. I take a huge breath of air. I open my eyes. The grass is still there. The sound of night. The light of the moon. I'm outside. The night. *Au clair de lune.* Lying in the grass. I'm in a field. I am in a field. Outside. The night. I must be dreaming. I'm not dreaming. I feel the grass. I see the moon. No. Impossible. They've let me go. They've tossed me in a field. I'm hallucinating. They could easily induce a hallucination. I sit up. Impossible. No more mattress. No more pitchers. No more concrete. No more grey. It's over. I grab a fistful of grass. I rip it out. It makes the sound of a fistful of grass being ripped out. I lift it to my nose. The smell of grass. I'm truly outside. No longer in a cell. I'm outside. Then I realize. No more Julian. I get up too fast. I look around. Julian. Who always wakes after I do. I scream. I howl. JULIAN! I start running. Everywhere. I shout. JULIAN! JULIAN! No, not that. JULIAN! I'm dizzy. My heart is racing. I'm breathing too fast. Julian. I'm free. I feel the wind on my cheeks. The grass under my feet. It's not cold. But Julian is not here. I'm free and Julian isn't with me. Tears start running down my cheeks. They've taken Julian away from me again. I'm free. I don't know his last name. I don't even know what city he lives in. I'm free and I can't find him. I fall to my knees. I hear the call of a bird. I'm crying. I'm free and I'm crying tears that hurt more than anything I've experienced. I whisper between sobs. A litany. Julian, Julian, Julian, Julian. Have they kept him? Have they freed him? Why me? Why not us? They can't do it. They can't take him away from me. I fall to the ground. My face against the grass. The bastards. I cry. It's the only thing I can do. I'm crying. I'm going to figure out a way to find him. I'm going to knock on every single door of every Julian in every city. But for now, I've had enough. I'm crying.

Then I hear it. Something. Far away. I hear my name. Julian. Shouting. Bellowing. He's just woken up. He's yelling my name. I get up. He's there. I shout. I'm running. I run towards his voice. Then I see him. Running towards me. We stop only a few feet from each other. Julian. He's here. We're here. We're free.

In his hand, he's holding something that looks like a business card. He holds it out to me. On it, in small black letters, I read:

The Rising Phoenix
Centre for the Rehabilitation of Human Kindness
Relearn the art of feeling, the art of living

And on the back, written in ink:

Don't relapse. We're watching.

Claudine Dumont is a writer, teacher, and photographer, and the co-owner of Ma Soeur et Moi café in Laval, Quebec. Visit her website at masoeuretmoicafe.com. *Captive* is her first novel.

David Scott Hamilton is a literary translator. *Exit*, his translation of Nelly Arcan's final novel, *Paradis, clef en main*, was shortlisted for the Governor General's Literary Award for Translation and named a *Globe and Mail* Top 100 Book. He lives in Montreal.